MW01223665

UNDER A WEEPING WILLOW

MARGARITA ESCOBAR

To my friends
Hans and Nancy
Thank you for
your support
Margarita

Content Notes

This work includes themes of murder, sexual assault and suicide that may be considered offensive to some readers.

Reader discretion is advised.

This book is a work of fiction. Names, characters and incidents are drawn from the author's imagination. Any resemblance to actual events or persons, living or dead, is entirely coincidental.

ISBN 978-1-7389777-0-3

Cover Design by Marie Mackay

No part of this book may be reproduced in any form or by any electronic or mechanical means, including information storage and retrieval systems, without written permission from the author, except for the use of brief quotations in a book review.

Copyright © 2023 by Margarita Escobar

All rights reserved.

CONTENTS

A SHORT STORY COLLECTION

A NOVELLA

To my grandfather, who taught me to love the written word.

A SHORT STORY COLLECTION

UP IN THE SKY

I'm fifteen, but I'll be sixteen in two months. Old enough to have some say in whether I want to see another stupid doctor. Not that they ever give me a choice. I'm sick and tired of my parents dragging me from place to place.

My mother says, "We're seeking someone to help us solve your problem."

What problem? I don't have a problem. I like to be left alone to do my shit, but that doesn't mean there's something wrong with me. Well, there was that suicide attempt, but that's in the past. I'm OK now. But my parents don't get it. If they would listen, they could've saved all the money they've spent on shrinks.

Tommy sat beside his parents, arms crossed over his

chest, lips tight. His deep brown eyes smouldered with fury. His narrow shoulders trembled in a contained rage. His father, a cardiologist, mirrored Tommy's posture, crossing his arms over his bulging abdomen.

His mother, a psychologist, sat beside her husband. Her right leg bounced with nervous intensity.

Tommy sneered and thought, *My father looks after hearts and my mother takes care of lost souls. Too bad they haven't been as successful with me. Not like Jess. She's the normal one, the perfect child.*

Despite his bitterness, Tommy liked his sister. She was pretty cool, as far as sisters went. She was fun to be around and she called things how she saw them. He always knew where he stood with Jess.

"You're a good guy, "she often said to him, "but kind of weird. Look at all the stupid stuff you read. Dostoevsky, Nietzsche, Hess. Could you be any more boring?"

He grimaced. "I don't care what you think. I like those books." A second later he asked, "But you like me, don't you?"

Jess giggled and ruffled his hair. "Sure, but only in my spare time."

His sister always made his heart feel lighter.

Tommy's musing was interrupted by the receptionist. "You may go in now."

Behind the imposing mahogany desk, Dr. Wilson leaned back in his comfortable

leather chair, waiting.

"Tommy, Joanna, Alfred, please take a seat," he said with an affable smile.

The boy had to force himself not to stare as the small mustache perched above Dr. Wilson's large mouth twitched with his words. "So, Tommy, tell me how are you doing?"

He rolled his eyes and looked around the room, fidgeting. "I'm fine, and you?"

Alfred shifted in his seat. Joanna pleaded, sounding upset, "Tommy, try to be polite."

"Both of you, please, take it easy," intervened Dr. Wilson. "Well, young man, you and I have known each other for a long time, right? I'm sure you know your parents and I want the best for you." He cleared his throat.

Dr. Wilson seems nervous. This must be bad news.

The doctor continued, confirming Tommy's suspicions. "That's why we think you should spend some time in our facility."

An invisible weight pressed upon the boy's chest, rendering him momentarily paralyzed. He squeaked out the words, "You what?" Wariness tightened his features. He understood "our facility" was a euphemism used to hide the nature of the place, as he saw it; a madhouse, an asylum, a psychiatric hospital. A place for crazy people.

They decide everything in my life like I'm a marionette and they pull the strings. I hate it. He dug his nails into his palms.

"You knew about this, Mother?" A knot twisted his gut. His mother had betrayed him.

"It's only for a short time, love," his mother said.

"Don't call me love," he replied.

The boy's tears edged his eyelids. He glanced out the window and tried to clear his mind. He concentrated on the magnolia tree blossoms, the petals fluttering in the gentle breeze.

"I think you'll benefit from this, Tommy. We have a good program for young people like yourself," said the doctor, his voice calm. As if that would somehow convince the boy what they were suggesting was a good thing.

He realized they'd already made up their minds. Eyes tightening, Tommy dropped his shoulders.

"Whatever," he muttered.

"Once you see our facility and experience the program, you'll be convinced it was a good decision," said Dr. Wilson.

His mother tried to touch his hand, but Tommy refused. The doctor rose from his seat, ending the meeting.

On the way home, the boy sat in the back seat, immersed in thoughts.

Tommy sensed something wasn't right with himself. *What's wrong with me? Why am I always sad? I hate going to school and the stupid jerks in my class. I'd like to go to sleep and never wake up. That would be cool.*

* * *

When they got home, Tommy went straight to his bedroom, slammed the door, and threw himself on the bed. Downstairs, his parents would decide his fate. He needed to overhear their conversation. He got up, descended the stairs, and tiptoed toward his parents' office. Staring at the partly open door ahead of him, he listened, his heart hammering.

"I just want a clear diagnosis." His father's voice sounded concerned.

"Honey, you must realize staying at the clinic is the best option for him," said his mother.

"I'm not so sure."

"You know he's been seen by the best specialists in Toronto, and all have said the same. Why are you not convinced?"

Looking through the half-open door,Tommy saw his father sitting in his desk chair, holding his head with both hands, defeated. Tommy's mother by his side. She squeezed her husband's shoulder and cried.

Tommy made his way back to his room. He slumped in a chair, rested his head on the back of it and closed his eyes.

Why do my parents think I'd be OK at the clinic? The truth is they don't want me around because I'm a pain in the neck. They want to get rid of me and send me away. I know they do.

He stood and paced his bedroom, thinking. The evening sent a warm breeze through his open window. Through it, he could see the pool, the tennis court, and the beautiful garden full of rose bushes, manicured shrubs and trees.

Sure, I could have anything I want, but I'm not happy. Not here. But there is a place where I'd feel content–in the clouds. Yeah, up in the sky. I'd like to be a bird and fly away. I don't know where, but far from here.

When he travelled with his parents by plane, Tommy loved to watch the clouds, which were like sculptures made of cotton wool. He imagined them as anything he wanted them to be: a wild horse running freely, a majestic raven flying high above a mountain peak, or a giant butterfly.

His thoughts drifted.

Well, maybe spending some time with other nuts like me won't be so bad. He packed a bag with clothing, ready for the next day, and went to his sister's room.

"What's up?" Jess asked while painting her toenails.

His sad demeanor touched his sister's heart, and she capped her nail polish. "Getting my shit ready to go to the madhouse," he said.

"Yeah, Mom told me about it. And don't be silly. It is not a madhouse. It's just a place to rest and get your head around stuff. That's all. And remember what I've always said, Tommy, if you don't open your mouth, you might pass for normal." She laughed at her joke.

"Now who's the silly one?" he asked, half smiling.

* * *

The first days at the clinic were difficult for Tommy. He couldn't get used to the routines, endless group sessions, and useless talks with Dr. Wilson. But after the first week, things got better. As part of the program, the boys were offered weekly outings to the city center.

He first saw her through a window while he walked down a busy street. She stared into space, her blue eyes enormous, her long dark hair framing the oval of her young face. She smiled slightly, her parted lips painted the soft pink of an early morning sky.

"She is so beautiful," he whispered, almost breathless. That night he couldn't sleep, thinking about the mysterious girl in the window.

I have to see her again or I'll die. I need to make sure it wasn't a dream.

Tommy kept going on the weekly outings with his group. Every time he saw the girl in the window, he felt his heart would escape from his chest with his overwhelming happiness. He didn't notice the girl was always at the same window, her expression unchanged. She didn't move and her smile never faded. But he didn't care. He fell in love with all the impulsiveness of his tender years and began to fantasize about how life would be with her.

I'm sure she'd be good for me and I could be happy with her in my life. I may even feel normal.

One day, while the group walked back to the clinic, he whispered to himself, "I have to do something." As his determination rose, he thought, "I must do it.

That night, Tommy planned his strategy. *I'm going to run away with her, take her to a safe place, and I'll see what to do next.*

On the next outing, Tommy gathered all the courage he could muster. He left the group and ran to the window where the girl was. Hidden in his jacket was, a hammer he'd taken from the janitor's closet the night before. With both hands, he grabbed the hammer and with the force of a cyclone broke the glass to pieces.

He took the girl in his arms and ran to the street.

In his desperate attempt to get away, he didn't notice a truck coming in the opposite direction. As the truck slammed into Tommy, the girl leapt from his hands, her plastic arms, and legs flying away from her trunk. The boy landed on his back, staring at the sky. He wasn't in any pain but felt a dense, warm fluid running down the back of his neck.

Tommy looked at the clouds with half-closed eyes. An incomparable sense of calm flooded his body; he felt light, almost ethereal.

A police officer arrived at the scene and found a boy lying on his back with a peaceful expression painted on his face. A pool of blood had seeped from his head. Tommy had no pulse.

Despite his many years in the police force, sympathy and sorrow came over him at the waste of such a young life.

The police officer shouted: "Get that mannequin off the road!"

In the cerulean sky amidst the clouds, a wild horse, a majestic raven and a giant butterfly watched from above.

A CHANCE ENCOUNTER

It was autumn in Madrid. A carpet of leaves, yellow, red, and all tones of brown, covered the ground. The bare trees stood guard as if watching over the people who rushed past, immersed in the bustle of the metropolis.

I worked a few shifts per week at a coffee shop to supplement my day job as a librarian. As usual, the place was filled with locals and students, some chatting, others working on their laptops.

A young girl put her hand up calling for service. I gathered my notepad and went over to take her order.

"What can I get you, miss?"

"I'll have a cappuccino, please." She glanced at my nametag. "Thank you, Laura."

The girl had a mysterious look about her. I estimated her to be in her early twenties,

perhaps a little older. Deep brown hair framed her hazel

eyes and made her olive skin glow. When she looked at me, I was wrenched into the past. It felt as if I were looking back at her through the eyes of my twenty-year-old self.

Then, as quickly as it had come, the feeling was gone. I turned to gather the cups from the table behind me.

When I got home, I couldn't stop thinking about the girl from the coffee shop. And

when I signed in to check my schedule for the week I realized it was October 28th, the day I lost my child and my childhood.

The next morning I got out of the shower and stood naked in front of the mirror. Almost forty. The past decade had stolen the firmness from my breasts and my hips but they'd kept their smoothness.

I should've been happy with my life. I spent my limited free time with a few good friends, wandering Madrid's museums, or reading my beloved books. However, there was a gapping, indescribable void in my heart, that, kept me awake for hours at night.

Sometimes, sitting on the ledge of my bedroom window, I would observe the birth of the new day and admire the colours of dawn. But not even that wonderful gift could dispel my deep, consuming sadness, a despair that had implanted itself in the twists and curves of my brain.

Tears came to my eyes. I blinked hard and tried to smile, forcing myself to think life could still be full of blessings. Putting on a colorful dress, I tied a red carnation to my hair and went to meet Antonio. It was Saturday, a day we usually spent together.

* * *

We met at the beautiful Park Retiro, the largest and lushest of Madrid's green spaces. Antonio looked handsome in his jeans and blue sweater. We said hello and he hugged me tightly. Even though our relationship began a year ago, whenever we kissed, I would blush as desire flooded through me. Antonio smiled shyly but said nothing.

At six feet, he towered over me. He had thick, gray-flecked dark hair, chocolate eyes framed by laugh lines, and a strong jaw dusted with salt-and-pepper stubble. Whenever he looked deeply into my eyes, goosebumps would rise along my skin. It was as though he could see beneath my clothes, beneath my skin, to my soul. His penetrating stare made me feel naked, almost as if I were standing there with nothing on. I liked it.

Despite holding Antonio close to my heart, I hadn't yet shared my secret with him.

When sadness and an inexplicable emptiness grabbed my throat with both hands, I knew

I could count on him to throw me a lifeline.

We spent the morning at a book fair at the *Paseo del*

Prado, en la calle Alcalá. There, we discovered all kinds of literary treasures, new and old. We found classics and works by unknown authors, books on poetry, fiction, religion, and politics.

I loved browsing through those old books; to touch them felt like a caress. I wondered how many eyes had toured their pages, how many lives had been touched by those lines, and how many emotions those words had evoked.

In the evening Antonio and I attended a workshop sponsored by the University of Madrid. When the participants shared their writing, I was enraptured. They were people of different ages and ethnicities, but all shared their love for the written word.

When the last person stood to read, I was surprised to hear the voice of the girl from the coffee shop. She stood, imposing, proud, and sovereign as a statue before the room.

The poem she read surprised us all. She was perhaps the youngest among those gathered, but her poetry showed deep insight and intensity. Anyone would have thought she possessed the life experience of an octogenarian.

I couldn't help myself, and I approached her."Hello there. I think your poem was breathtaking."

"Thanks...Laura, right? I remember you from the coffee shop. I'm Erga." She smiled at me.

"Yes. I remember you too. What a coincidence! Do you come here often?"

"Yeah, I try if I'm not too busy with school."

Other people came to talk to her. "Sorry, maybe I'll see you at the coffee shop."

"Sure. See you around," I said and she went back to talk to the others.

When we left the workshop, *la luna de Madrid,* bright and enchanting, shone down upon us. Antonio laid his arm across my shoulders and we walked, like so many anonymous couples. When we reached my building, we went up to my apartment, had a few drinks, and went to bed. After lovemaking, I sat by my window ledge and gazed at the stars like I did so many sleepless nights. He woke and came to my side kissing my naked shoulder.

"Are you OK, honey?" he asked.

"Yes, love. I'm fine."

He touched my face and kissed my forehead. "We've been together for over a year. I think I know you well enough, and you're not OK."

My eyes welled with tears.

"You carry around a sadness that you can't deny. Do you want to share it with me?"

I wept softly.

He held me for a moment, stroking my hair. "I'm here, honey, let it all out."

I took a deep breath. "There is a thing about my past you don't know."

"OK, but I want you to know, whatever it is you need to tell me, it won't change what I feel for you. I love you, you know."

I gathered courage from deep within my soul. "I had a daughter when I was a teenager," I said with a quavering voice.

His eyes widened."What happened to her?"

"She died at birth." My voice broke. "Her birthday is approaching." I could no longer control my emotions and I sobbed. He cuddled me until my tears slowed.

"Where is your baby buried? You may want to go to her resting place if that helps."

"I don't know," I said through my tears.

"That's OK, my love," he said. His soothing voice calmed me.

He rocked me in his arms, the way a mother would rock a baby. He didn't say another word. I didn't want him to. I only needed his warmth.

* * *

The following morning, while working at the café, I spotted Erga, writing at a table. I approached her.

"Hello, Laura," she said, wearing an enchanting smile.

"Hello. It's nice to see you. I know you are busy and I have to go back to work. I just wanted to say hi," I said.

"Good to see you too." She returned to her task.

As time went by, she came into the café more often, so I decided to invite her to my

place. We spent a pleasant afternoon eating churros and drinking hot chocolate. She told me she studied literature at the University of Madrid and lived with two other girls, near the campus. She talked about her family, and even showed me a picture of her parents. They were a good-looking couple, with blond hair, fair complexions, and blue eyes.

Even though I saw Erga frequently, we didn't speak much, because she was always focused on her writing. One morning I sneaked a sandwich from the kitchen to give to her. "I want you to take this for your lunch break. It's on me," I said.

She gave me a surprised look, took the sandwich with a timid smile, and said, "Thanks, Laura, you're kind."

Her smile made my day.

One afternoon, after she left the café, I did something irrational. I followed her to find out where she lived. When she entered an apartment building, I hid behind a bush and waited. Shortly after, she walked out onto her second-floor balcony to water some plants.

* * *

I waited until next Sunday to find my way to the girl's place. There I stood, facing Erga's door, gathering the courage to knock. Finally, I did.

When she opened the door, her eyes bulged."Laura, what are you doing here?"

"Hello," I said twisting my fingers. "May I come in?"

"Sorry, sure. Come in."

I looked around the tiny apartment. A table full of books, a couple of chairs, a small TV, a worn-out couch and a kitchenette gave the impression of a student's place.

Erga cleared a spot on the couch. "Please, have a seat."

I sat, my hands on my lap.

She sat by my side, her forehead creased. "How did you know where I live?"

"I followed you last week," I said, my cheeks burning.

"What? Why did you do that?" She stood and backed away.

"I don't know. I don't have a coherent answer. Please, don't get upset with me," I pleaded.

"I don't appreciate people nosing around, Laura. If you wanted to visit me, you should have asked me first."

My head dropped to my chest. After a few seconds, I faced her. "I'm so sorry to have disturbed you, but I consider you a friend, in spite of the age difference."

"What are you trying to say?" She searched my face.

"Just what I said. I want to hang around with you. We could go to the movies or take a walk in the park. I don't know. Whatever you want to do—I'll be happy to be close to you."

Erga frowned, scrunching up her brow. "Are you coming on to me?"

"No, no nothing like that! Please, don't take me wrong. I could be your mother."

"Yes, but you're not."

"I'm so sorry about this misunderstanding." I struggled to hold back tears.

"It's fine. Please don't cry." She put a hand on my shoulder.

Her touch was comforting. It made me feel understood despite her not knowing

about the pain nested in my heart.

"Laura?" Her voice was quiet. I think you should go now.

* * *

Weeks went by. I looked out the window as the last autumn leaves covered the ground. As the season passed, my sadness grew. Erga wasn't coming into the café anymore.

As always, winter arrived with its bare trees and desolate gardens. One rainy morning, I received a phone call from my parents, in Seville.

"Hello?"

"Happy birthday!" My parents spoke into the phone at the same time.

"Oh! *Muchas gracias.*" I'd completely lost track of the days.

"Will you come for dinner? Next Friday and the weekend?"

After talking to my parents, I agreed and planned my trip

south. They lived in Triana, a beautiful Seville town, where they owned a picturesque pottery shop, filled with handcrafted earthenware, a popular industry in the area.

* * *

As I approached the shop's main entrance, I spotted my parents through the huge windows. They didn't see me coming, so I could observe them for a few minutes.

My father sat hunched over his computer, while my mother dusted a beautiful blue vase that sat on a shelf at the back of the room.

I saw a sweet-looking old woman, small and fragile. When I was a child, my mother seemed very tall. I remembered her flying around our house, like a butterfly, almost ethereal. She was always busy with things to do, making my early childhood the golden age I kept in my memories. How could anyone shrink so much?

I walked into the shop and hugged my mom from behind. Surprised, she turned, and we embraced.

As I held her, I was shocked by the change in her body since I'd last seen her. Her bony chest pressed against mine, her arms, delicate twigs that wrapped around me. I was sure I could've lifted her without much effort.

After my parents closed their shop for the day, we drove to their home, a welcoming place on a quiet street.

My old neighbourhood hadn't changed much. Some of

the houses had kept their original colors, and the trees were a little taller.

In spite of the season, my parents' front yard was filled with perennials and green splendour. Spring would transform their garden with a plethora of colorful flowers. Just as it did when I was a little girl.

After dinner, I sat beside my mother."I need to talk to you about something important, something that has been gnawing at me for a long time."

"What is this all about, love?" she said and put down her book.

"It's about my past, Mom."

Looking at her, I noticed her pallid face. She set her jaw and dropped her gaze to her knees. I guessed she sensed what I wanted to talk about.

The words came pouring out of my mouth, strong, fierce, and powerful. I spoke from my heart. I told her that since my daughter's death, I have had no peace, and now a feeling of anguish, impossible to overcome, threatened to consume me.

"Mom, I need to know where my baby is buried," I said, resolute.

"There is no use brooding over the past, darling," she said.

"I need to know, Mama, *por favor.*" I held back tears.

Mom kept quiet for a few minutes, which seemed an eternity. She moved closer and put her arm around me.

Her voice broke when she said, "Oh, *amor*, I don't know how to say this."

Hands trembling, she took mine in hers. She looked at me earnestly, angst painted on her face. "Your daughter didn't die."

I thought my heart would stop beating. But it didn't. Its thump resonated in my ears.

Before I could utter a word, she added. "Your baby was given in adoption."

I couldn't believe her words. "What? Oh, no, what are you saying? I've spent half of my life mourning a daughter who is alive? How could you, Mother?"

Mom covered her face with her hands and sobbed.

"I'm so sorry. You were a child yourself when she was born. You weren't ready to raise a baby," she said when she could talk. She added, "Your father and I thought it was the best thing to do. We wanted to protect you."

Stomach-churning, I didn't answer. My voice had left me.

"Please, try to understand, Laura. Maybe what we did was a mistake, but we did it because we love you. It was for your own good," she said and touched my arm. I jerked it away.

"You did it for me?" I raised my voice. A wave of nausea engulfed me. "Liar!" I shouted. "You did it for you because it would have been an inconvenience to help me raise my daughter." My throat tightened.

"No, no, baby, you're mistaken," she pleaded.

I wanted to slap her, but I contained myself and walked out.

I ran upstairs to my old bedroom, threw myself on the bed and sobbed until I fell asleep.

* * *

When I woke up, it was night already. I didn't want to go downstairs to face my mother. I needed time to think about what had happened.

I pondered things and tried to put myself in my mother's position. What would I have done in her place? I searched for an answer but couldn't come up with any.

I looked around at my old doll collection, school certificates, and prizes. Nostalgia invaded my soul. Mom kept everything as it was when I left home.

Pity for my mother swept over me. I realized she loved me then as much as she does now. Maybe my parents did what they thought was best for me.

I picked up my bags and went to look for her.

She was sitting in her rocking chair in the lounge, her head cocked to one side. Her fingers rested intertwined over her abdomen and her eyes looked at a distant point. I sat beside her.

"Could you forgive me one day?" she asked in a thin voice and wiped a tear from her face.

"I will try, Mom. Please, tell me about my baby," I begged.

"She was beautiful. The couple who adopted her couldn't have children. They were ready to be parents. I believe she had a good life."

As Mother pronounced those words, I prayed for forgiveness to come. I knew I had a long way to go, but first I had to feel strong again.

* * *

I moved through the next day at the café on the verge of tears. It was all so unbelievable.

"Laura?"

I looked up from a table I was cleaning and into Erga's face.

"I just wanted to say hello. I haven't been around because I'm writing exams." She looked into my eyes.

"It's good to see you." My heart raced.

"I'm not happy with the way we parted last time when you visited my place. Sorry if I hurt you."

Her voice sounded so sincere, so honest.

"Thank you, but it's my fault," I said. "I'm sorry I intruded on you. I was not myself. Can you forgive me?"

"There is nothing to forgive," she said with a luminous smile.

I'd like to imagine that my daughter, wherever she is, may find a friend as wonderful as Erga.

THE BRIDGE

Carmen added a final touch to her outfit—a white carnation in her hair. Esteban's favorite flower. She fluffed her skirt once more and left the apartment. Her heart galloped in her chest as she rushed to the park. Sunny skies filled her soul with joy and anticipation.

She hurried to her destination. Fidgeting with her blouse and her jean jacket, she sat on their bench and waited for Esteban to appear beside the little bridge over the creek. He never came close, but she knew he'd show up, just as he has done every Tuesday for the last ten months.

She fondly remembered the first time they met. It was at the university library one Saturday morning; she thought she was the only crazy person to go to the library on weekends, but she needed to work on a paper. It was her last year before finishing her teaching degree.

She spotted him hunched over a book, taking notes. When he realized he was being observed, he smiled at her. She blushed, but she held his gaze.

He gathered his books and made his way to Carmen's spot. "Hi," he said. "Would you mind if we share this table?"

Before she could utter a word, he grabbed a chair and sat facing her. From the first moment, his hazel eyes captivated Carmen's heart. Their attraction was mutual.

All that happened after—falling in love, moving in together and their graduation— ran across Carmen's mind like slides or images spinning quickly on a projector.

As sometimes happens in life, beautiful things don't last long enough.

* * *

Warmth radiating throughout her body, she checked her watch again. Just a few minutes to wait. At six o'clock exactly Esteban stood by the side of the bridge. It wasn't him in full flesh, just his image. But his eyes glimmered, as they had the first day they met.

Because he was transparent, Carmen could see through him. Literally. She glimpsed at a mother pushing a stroller, a kid running after a ball and an elderly couple trudging along the pathway. She wanted that moment to last forever, but she understood it wasn't possible. Gratitude to have a little time to glance at Esteban's eyes invaded her soul.

Then, gradually, like the sun going down on the horizon,

he disappeared.

"Until next Tuesday, my love," she whispered.

Content, she smiled and stood, grabbed her bag and went back to her place.

Carmen didn't talk to anyone about her dates with Esteban. It was her secret. She didn't want people to think she was losing her mind.

But, sometimes secrets find their way into the light.

* * *

The following week, she was having lunch in her school's staff room. The kids' laughter from the playground drifted through the open windows. She loved children and enjoyed being a teacher.

"Hi Carmen," Mario said. "May I sit beside you? I hate eating alone."

"Sure."

"How are things going with you?" he asked.

"Good, I love Tuesdays."

"May I ask why?"

"Can't tell. It's a secret."

"I'm your friend. I'm good at keeping secrets."

"Well, if you insist. I have a date on Tuesdays."

He stared at Carmen. "Are you serious?"

"Very much so," she said.

Mario put his sandwich down. "After Esteban's passing and all you've been through, I'm glad you're going out."

She inspected her hands and kept silent.

He continued, "I loved him very much. He was my best friend, more like a brother. But he's gone, and you are here."

A cheerless expression appeared in her eyes. "I miss him, you know?"

Mario touched her hand. "I miss him too."

"I'm going to tell you something special," she said.

"Please, do."

"I've seen Esteban."

"Do you see him in your dreams? That'd be understandable."

"No, not in my dreams. I have been meeting him every Tuesday at six, at Alameda Park."

An incredulous gaze flashed across Mario's face. He sighed. "I don't know what to say."

"You think I am out of my mind, don't you?"

"No. If you tell me you can see him, I believe you. How do you see him?" he asked.

"I don't see him like he was. I see his image."

"What do you mean?"

"I see through him, something like a clear silhouette, but not exactly. The only real thing is his eyes. He looks at me. I know he does.

"Does he talk to you?"

"No, he doesn't. I see him at a distance."

Mario smiled."I'm glad seeing him makes you happy."

"I knew you'd understand." A brief smile appeared on her face.

For a moment, Mario closed his eyes, breathing her pleasant scent.

"Thank you for listening," she said.

"Anytime. I have to go back to class," he replied and left.

* * *

Time dragged for Carmen. Tuesdays took forever to arrive. Sometimes she saw Mario in the staff room.He casually whispered in her ear, "How is Esteban's image looking?"

"It's beautiful, as always," she answered.

As days passed, unexpected things happened. When Carmen got to their bench in the park and saw Esteban's image, it wasn't as clear as usual. Did he look at her? She couldn't tell. Feeling disappointed, she went home.

The following Tuesday something extremely rare occurred. He was late. She waited for half an hour before Esteban materialized. This time the image was blurrier than the week before. She was certain he didn't look at her.

That night, she cried herself to sleep.

She saw Mario at lunch break "You look beautiful today, but so sad." She didn't know why she blushed, and gave him a half-smile but didn't engage in conversation.

* * *

Another Tuesday came, and Carmen arrived at the park on time. She waited for an hour; then two hours turned into three. Esteban didn't come to their date. It was already

dark when she got home. She slumped onto her couch, a dejected expression settled on her face.

The following, day she didn't go to work. She couldn't. Her puffy eyes gave away a night of solid crying. She couldn't understand what was going on. Why was Esteban breaking her heart?

She didn't see Mario at work. She asked around, but a colleague said he had taken a week off. Too bad. She missed having someone to talk to during her lunch break.

* * *

Carmen had been going to the park, every Tuesday for the past year. When she approached their bench, a foreboding uncertainty filled her heart. She had a premonition about Esteban's image. She was right. He didn't show up.

For some unknown reason, she didn't feel as sad as she expected.

When she looked at the little bridge over the creek, Mario stood there smiling. Her heart pounded an erratic rhythm.Throat thickening with emotion, she waved.

He approached her bench."Hello...I knew where to find you." Without waiting for an answer, he said, "I have a couple of tickets for the movies. Would you like to come with me?"

His eyes, full of anticipation, gave Carmen the confidence she needed to answer without hesitation. "I'd love to."

A GOOD DEED

Pam turned off her computer and tidied up her desk. Heavy rain splattered the windows; strong winds bent the trees in the nearby park. As a legal assistant, she worked for a small family practice law firm. She didn't bring home a substantial salary, but it paid the bills. Things were tight for her and Cory, her-five-year-old son. After a messy divorce, she tried to juggle work and child-rearing on her own. Before leaving the building, she called home.

An elderly voice answered.

"Hi, Rose, how's Cory doing?" she asked.

"Hi, Pam, he's fine. He finished his dinner already."

"I'm so sorry to be late, but I had a mountain of paper-work to finish. I hate not having dinner with him. Please, put him on."

Hi, Mommy, when are you coming home?" a tiny voice ɹed.

"Hi, sweetheart, how're you?"

"Good. I ate dinner already. I miss you."

"I'll be home as soon as I can and we could read your favourite book. I promise."

"Okay, mommy. I love you every day."

"Me too, sweetheart, very much." Her voice broke after hearing Cory's candid remark.

"Don't worry," Rose said, sounding sympathetic. "We're fine. Drive carefully. It looks like a deluge is unfolding out there."

"I will. See you soon."

* * *

While driving, she regretted living in the country. It took her almost an hour to get to her place. As a writer, Steven, her ex-husband, used to work from home. He convinced her it was a good thing to live in touch with nature, away from the rush of the big city. But it wasn't her choice; like everything else in their marriage, he had the last word. When Cory turned three, Steve left home and moved away with his lover.

The rain got heavier. It was dark. Pam could hardly see the road. She steadied her hands on the steering wheel and focused on her driving.

Suddenly, she slammed on the brakes. Someone was on the road. Pam squinted and her heart skipped a beat. In front of her car, a young woman stood waving her hands in the air. Soaked to the bone, the stranger ran to the car's passenger side.

Pam rolled down the window. "Are you okay?" She took in the stranger's appearance: a lanky girl, wearing jeans and only a T shirt, standing in the rain. Water painted her breasts on the tee. Her crying young face dripped water and tears.

"Please, lady, help me," the girl pleaded, wringing her top with shaking hands.

Pam opened the passenger's side door and let her in. The girl couldn't stop shivering.

"Hi, what's your name?" Pam asked.

"I'm Kelly," the girl said. "Thank you for stopping."

"I'm Pam. I've got a towel in the gym bag back there," she said, pointing to the

back seat. "Get it to dry yourself a bit. What happened to you?" The girl started to cry and couldn't utter a word.

"That's okay, calm down now. Where do you live? I could take you home." Pam noticed the girl's green hair and the large ring she wore in her nose. "How old are you, anyway?"

"I'm sixteen. I live close by, but I won't go home." Her voice sounded determined. She dried her face and hair with the towel.

Pam frowned. "Why not?"

"My mother is dating an asshole. He tried to get into my pants, so I ran away."

"You should've called the police."

"I didn't have time. I just got out of the house and ran onto the road."

"I'm sorry that happened to you."

"Why don't you phone your mom and talk to her?"

"No way. I did the first time it happened, but she didn't believe me. She's crazy

about that guy."

"What are you going to do?"

"I don't know yet." Kelly buried her head in her hands.

Pam squeezed the girl's shoulder. "Okay, I'll take you to my place, and then we'll

figure out what to do."

She restarted the car and drove about a block when Kelly's scream startled her.

"Stop, please, stop! A log, a log! Watch out!"

"What happened?" I didn't see a thing. "Oh, God, it's so frigging dark." A sheen of sweat formed on Pam's forehead, cheek, and chin. Her hands shook uncontrollably.

"What are we going to do?" Kelly asked.

"Help me to move the log. Let's do it together," Pam said.

The two women got out of the car, maneuvered the log and cleared the road. They ran back to the vehicle. As Pam started the car, a face appeared in the rearview mirror.

The man wearing a hoodie came out of his hiding place.

Pam turned her head to face the intruder. Panic gripped her heart.

"Who are you? What are you doing here?" She clutched the steering wheel in fright. "What do you want?"

She felt the cold metal on her neck. The blade of a carving knife rested against her throat.

"Don't you move, bitch. Do what you are told and you'll be fine."

"Please, don't hurt us," Pam pleaded. She couldn't stop shaking.

"Keep driving," the stranger said. He put away the knife.

Kelly had not said a word since the man got in the car.

While driving, Pam glanced at the stranger through the rearview mirror. He wore a black beanie and his gaze darted right and left. An incipient black mustache sat on his upper lip. She thought he could be in his late teens or early twenties. He smelled of weed.

* * *

Pam kept driving for a while longer. She squirmed on her seat.

Kelly and the man exchanged looks.

"Stop the car," the man said.

"What do you want?" Pam's voice trembled.

"Get out of the car," he commanded.

She did. Her legs shook so hard she wasn't sure she could stand. Her heart

pounded in her chest. Rain poured down her face. She wanted to say something, but not a word escaped her mouth.

"We are taking your car," Kelly said, standing by the man's side.

"Oh God, you are in on this? I can't believe it!"

"Now you know." Kelly pulled a stick of gum out of her pocket and popped it in her mouth.

A thick forest lined the roadside. It was dark, and the rain hadn't eased off. Suddenly, the man kicked Pam on the back of her knee. She fell to the ground.

"Stop, Trev, no need to hurt her," Kelly said.

Trevor, oblivious to Kelly's remark, dragged Pam to the side of the road, punched her in her gut and pushed her. The blow left her breathless. The way the land dropped made Pam slide down a steep slope.

"Hurry up, get in the car!" he yelled at Kelly. She jumped into the passenger seat and they drove off.

On her way down the slope, Pam suffered cuts and bruises in her face and, her lower lip bled. Twigs and mud nested in her tangled hair. Darkness engulfed her. She attempted to get up, but she slid farther down. In her head Cory's tiny voice kept calling her back home.

After several attempts, a burst of twisted roots and some thick branches helped her to drag herself up to the side of the road.

* * *

The rain had slowed down. There were no cars around. Shivering, teeth chattering, Pam sat on a rock waiting for a car to pass by. It seemed she was sitting on that cold stone forever when she spotted a car's headlights. She sprung from her seat and ran into the middle of the road. Hands in the air, she shouted, "Stop, stop, help!" The car braked in front of her, its high beams blinding her. For a few seconds, she couldn't see clearly.

A man got out of the car and ran to her. "Are you hurt?"

Pam could hardly stand, and she felt dizzy, everything was spinning. The last thing she remembered was a stranger approaching her. When she opened her eyes, she was lying down in the man's car. His jacket covered her up to her chin.

"Where am I?"

"You're in my car. You passed out, and I brought you here," he said.

She placed a hand on her forehead. "Thank you. I'm Pam."

"I'm Michael. What happened to you?"

Pam's voice sounded weak, and her eyes became watery. " A couple of teens assaulted me. They stole my car."

Michael shook his head. "Did you call the police?"

"I will, as soon as I get to my house. They took my purse. I don't have a phone. I live close by. Could you take me home, please?"

"For sure."

He started the car and as he drove, Pam observe him. He had angular features, a well-kept mustache, and abundant white hair. A pair of gold-rimmed glasses gave him the look of a teacher, Pam thought. "What do you do for a living, Michael"?

"I'm a math teacher."

Pam smiled.

"Do you think you could recognize the teens who attacked you?"

"I believe so. The girl had bright green hair. She got in the car first and the young man got in later. He put a log in the road to make me stop. They knew each other. I guess they must've planned the assault together."

He frowned when he asked, "Did she have a nose ring?"

"As a matter of fact, yes, she did."

Michael stopped the car. He sucked in a quick breath. "My daughter is sixteen. She dyes her hair bright green, and she wears a ring on her nose. Her name is Kelly."

Pam's mouth fell open. "Oh!" she gasped. Not knowing what else to do, she touched Michael's shoulder. "I'm sorry."

"Yeah, me too. She's our only child. She lies all the time. She runs away with trashy boys and then returns home. We've been to counselling countless times. My wife and I don't know what to do with her anymore."

Pam didn't say a word.

Michael continued. "Too bad kids don't come with a manual when we bring them home from the maternity ward."

She gave an understanding nod.

"I'm sorry your daughter turned out this way. But she's young, and there is time to amend her mistakes. What do we do now?"

"You do what you have to," he said.

She bit her lower lip."I think I should call the police."

"Yeah, I agree. It's the right thing to do. Kelly is a minor, and this is her first offense. Probably, she'll have to do community work. Even if she has to spend a couple of nights in jail; it'd be good for her."

Michael continued, "I'm sorry for what you went through."

"Thanks. Me too."

"I think I should take you to your place."

"Yes, please, do." She gave him a half—smile.

As Pam walked through the front door, a sense of relief came over her. She made her way to Cory's bedroom. Her child slept peacefully, holding his stuffed animal; she moved close. She wiped her tears with her thumbs and kissed his forehead.

Cory woke up. "Why are you crying, Mommy?" She just shook her head and smiled.

A Cabin by the Lake

"Honey, I'm ready to leave," Sandra said while closing her bags. John came into the bedroom. "So, where is this mysterious cabin of yours?"

"It's not mine. It belongs to my friend Kate."

"Fine, I'll take your bags downstairs, but I still don't get why you want to go alone."

"I've told you already."

"Yeah, Barb wants you to finish your novel," he said, mocking a female voice.

"John, don't be like that, please."

"Sorry, hon, but I miss you already." He hugged her from behind rubbing his pelvis against her buttocks.

"Oh, love, stop it," she moaned.

But he didn't. Taking his time, he caressed her breasts and unbuttoned her blouse. Her nipples swelled under his fingertips. He pushed her gently onto the bed and ran his hand under her skirt, between her inner thighs, to find her wet and ready.

Loud groans escaped her throat as he entered her roughly, the way she liked it. After that, tiny pieces of sun exploded beneath her eyelids. When their loving finished, she rested her head in the hollow of his elbow.

He turned around, and kissed her on the lips, asking over her mouth, "When are you going to marry me?"

She giggled softly. "Soon, my love, soon".

Sandra stood beside the car until John closed the trunk.

Her abundant auburn hair danced in the strong wind, as cloudy skies suggested a summer rain.

"Come here, my princess." He grabbed her by the waist.

She buried her face in his neck, closing her eyes to savour the recent memory of their lovemaking.

"I'm so lucky to have you in my life," she whispered before he kissed her deep and hard.

He always smells so good. His aftershave drives me insane, or is it his skin's natural aroma that drives me wild?

"Drive carefully," he said while waving a hand at the moving car.

"Don't worry," she shouted. Looking into her rearview mirror, John's figure gradually diminished. She turned on the music and drove onto the main road.

He watched her go and sighed. *I'm relieved to have the*

place to myself before Jenny arrives. Later we'll go to that house she told me about.

* * *

Endless forests, majestic mountains, and abundant wildflowers adorned the meadows. Sandra imagined a talented artist may have painted such a magnificent landscape. Coming back from her reverie, the lake appeared on her right. She marveled and

rejoiced at its vast beauty.

When Sandra got to the cabin, the rain had slowed. The main door was unlocked, as her friend Kate said it would be. She liked her friend's cabin. The living area had an ample couch, a couple of sitting chairs, and a large standing lamp. A pleasant aroma from a bouquet of fresh flowers on a side table filled the room. That was Kate and her delicate details.

She took her bags to the guest bedroom, put her toiletries case in the bathroom and went to the kitchen to make herself a cup of coffee. Fatigue took hold of her, and she couldn't keep her eyes open. She left her coffee unfinished and went to bed.

The next morning, she woke up to a ray of sun sneaking through the window curtain, caressing her face. Holding her first cup of coffee, she entered the living room and sat facing the main window.

The lake, with its deep blue water, seemed like an endless blanket of serene beauty, reflecting the indigo sky above. She needed a few days to write and relax. Too many stressors in her life made it difficult to be productive.

Her writing started in her early forties, almost ten years ago. Maybe a bit too late to pursue this new adventure, she sometimes thought, but she had to do it. She had never regretted her decision.

Still in her pajamas, she stepped outside to the deck. Even though summer was almost over, the sapphire blue sky promised a sunny day. She took a deep breath and her lungs expand with fresh air.

Sandra glanced across the lake. A fancy-looking home with an old oak tree, manicured lawns, well-maintained gardens, and an attractive water feature caught her eye. *It must be nice to own a place like that*, she thought.

She went back inside and sat on the large couch facing the lake, to finish her coffee. A pair of binoculars on the window ledge got her attention. She stared at them for a few seconds, but her observation got interrupted by her phone beeping.

"Sandra? How is your writing going?" Her editor's voice sounded enthusiastic.

"Good morning, Barb. Isn't that the right thing to say if you call someone early in the morning?"

"Oh, don't be so snappy. How are you?"

"I'm fine. Got here yesterday afternoon. I'll start working as soon as we finish talking."

"I don't have to tell you we are racing against time, right?" Barb emphasized the word *right*.

"Yeah, so don't."

"I don't want to be a nag, Sandra. But you know we have deadlines."

"Yes, sorry. I promise I'll finish the last draft this weekend."

"Fine. I'll call you later. Happy writing, darling."

Sandra let out a long sigh of relief and put her phone on silent.

She spent most of the day writing furiously. Her novel came out as a story of love, betrayal, and murder. By nightfall, she was exhausted, so she made another coffee and sat on the deck. A full moon illuminated the sky, giving her a clear vision of her surroundings. The fancy house across the lake piqued her curiosity once more.

I wonder who lives there?

She was too tired to keep guessing, so she went to bed.

* * *

The next morning she woke almost at midday. After a quick shower, she got her coffee ready and went to sit on the big couch facing the lake. Her eyes rested again on the

binoculars on the window ledge.

I know it's not nice to peek at people, she thought while sipping her coffee *but what the heck? No one will know.*

She put her drink down and grabbed the binoculars. She focused her vision on the house across the lake. Sandra spotted someone reclined on a chaise under the shadow of a large oak tree. She thought it could be a man, but she wasn't sure, because the tree trunk obstructed part of her view.

A stunning young woman wearing a minuscule red bikini walked toward the

chaise, removed her top, giggled, and threw it into the air.

Sandra felt uneasy, but a faint smile appeared on her face. She put the binoculars down.

What a scene. I'd better finish up my drink and stop spying on young lovers.

* * *

Under the shade of the oak tree, the couple on the chaise embraced passionately. "Oh love, I've missed you so much," she whispered in his ear.

"Not as much as I, baby."

"I'm happy to be house-sitting this place. Isn't it grand? Rich people know how to live well." Jenny added, "But the main reason I like it here is it gives us a chance to spend time together, away from everything. We don't see each other as often as I wish." Her tone sounded like a reproach.

"I know, honey, I feel the same way, but we have to be patient. We'll have a lifetime to spend together. Remember that."

"Yeah, you've been telling me the same thing for how long already? " She stood and got a towel to cover herself.

"Please, let's not argue."

"I'm tired of waiting."

"I promised you, baby. We won't have to wait too long. When I marry her, I'll have access to her money."

* * *

Sandra woke early and picked up her laptop, her notes, and a coffee to start work. She stared at the blank page. Her mind went places—her work, her writing, and John. Always him in her heart. She welcomed that thought. Smiling tenderly, she let her mind reminisce about him.

She recalled how he stormed into her life, without waiting for an invitation, breaking down the walls that had enclosed her heart and taking up residence there. Since they'd moved in together, her life had changed for the better. Despite her mother saying that John was after the money her father left her, she loved him, and that was enough.

Being twenty-five years older than John bothered her at the beginning, but not anymore. She turned fifty a month ago, but being in John's arms made her feel young again. Her memories drifted as her fingers danced over the laptop keys, following the rhythm of her thoughts.

After a while, she let out a long sigh of relief, rubbed her temples, and stood. On her laptop screen, two words glittered like shining stars: THE END. She jumped up and down, like a child after opening birthday presents. With the back of her hand, she wiped away a few tears.

That's it. I'm done. My last draft is finished. The first thing

I need to do is call John, to share my good news. I'll call Barb later.

She grabbed her phone and called. No answer—only his voicemail.

That's bizarre–he told me he wasn't going anywhere today. Oh, well, maybe he's showering.

She left a message. "Hi, honey, good morning. Call me when you can. Love you and miss you."

* * *

Jenny turned around on the bed to face the man she just made love with. He slept soundly. She took the time to observe his features, his blond curls resting on his face,

his full-lipped mouth, his strong jaw.

She decided he was a good-looking guy, even cute, but she wasn't crazy about him. The fact he could get a good chunk of money when the time was right made her smile. She got up quietly and went to the bathroom.

His phone beeping woke John up. Half asleep, he listened to Sandra's message.

"Crap," he muttered. Quickly he got out of bed, grabbed his jeans, and called her back.

"Morning, honey. Sorry I didn't hear your call. I was in the shower."

"That's okay, love. How are you?"

"I'm bored without you."

"Well, I've got good news. I'm done with my last draft. I'll be home early."

His mouth fell open. "Are you coming home today?"

"You don't sound too happy about it."

"Don't be silly. Of course, I'm happy, honey. I'll make reservations for our favorite restaurant, to celebrate you finishing your draft."

"Great! That sounds good, love."

John ran his slick palms along the side of his jeans.

Now, I'm in trouble, he thought. *Jenny is going to have a fit over me cutting our weekend short. And I have to hurry up to get back home before Sandra does. Shit, what a mess.*

As Sandra drove back to her place, her mind couldn't focus on anything else but the man she loved.

Sandra and John finished dinner at the restaurant. While waiting for dessert, his foot tapped an irritating off-beat rhythm, alerting her of his mood. As usual, she picked up the check.

"You seem distracted tonight. Something wrong?" she asked.

"No, of course not darling. I'm just a bit preoccupied with financial issues, that's all."

"How many times should I tell you not to worry about it? You know you can count on me. Do you need some money?"

"Thanks, but no. I have to figure this out on my own."

"Okay, but don't sweat about it. Promise me you'll tell me if things get rough."

"I will love, I promise."

On their way home, they didn't talk much. His love-making that night was hurried and mechanical. Hands on the back of his neck, John stared at the ceiling, mulling over what to do next while she slept comfortably at his side.

* * *

The following morning, Sandra finished preparing breakfast and went to their bedroom to get John. While in the shower, his phone beeped. It was unlocked. She thought for a moment to take the phone and bring it to him, but when she saw the name Jenny displayed on the screen, her curiosity made her stop. With trembling hands, she picked up the phone and read the message. "Call me. Need to hear your voice." As if in a trance, she couldn't stop herself from checking the phone.

A picture of a young girl, wearing a minuscule red bikini, standing in front of a fancy house with manicured gardens, smiled at her from the screen.

Sandra's heartbeat raced and a lump rose in her throat. She put the phone down. Piercing pain in the middle of her chest made it hard to breathe.

Who was the girl? And why was her picture on John's phone?

The answer was obvious. Sandra wiped a tear, swallowed hard, and painted on a fake smile.

John came into the bedroom wearing a towel around his waist. He grabbed her and swirled her around, asking over her mouth, "How is my princess doing?"

"I'm good, hon. Just a bit tired, I didn't sleep well."

"Sorry to hear that. Do you have a minute?" he asked while he started to undo her blouse.

"No, not this time. I said I was tired." She shot him a stern look.

The corners of John's eyes creased with worry, but he dismissed it with a childish smile. "I understand, honey. I need to do some errands, and then we could go out for lunch, if that's okay with you."

"Sure."

The man she loved had made fun of her and hurt her deeply. *He has to pay for it, and he will*, she thought.

A couple of days went by. Sandra pretended nothing unusual had happened between them. But in her head, revenge brewed. Despite the unbearable pain and hate that filled her heart, she could still think straight enough to plan her vengeance.

Time crept along, like a cold reptile, on that ominous day. Inescapably, night arrived. Sandra was ready for what she had to do. She was aware of John's routine. He usually took a bath before going to bed. That would give her a chance to execute her plan.

She wished she had a pistol, but she didn't.

Sandra took a deep breath, grabbed her hairdryer and opened the bathroom door. Quietly, she approached the tub.

As she expected, John had dozed off submerged with the water up to his chin. He had taken his last bath.

TOO LATE

Once again, Christine eyed the envelope trembling in her hand. She pressed it to her chest and gazed through the window at an endless white carpet.

Alberta's winters seemed eternal. The sky was somber, menacing, and ominous. Dark clouds rambled around its vastness like obscure ghosts.

Despite the gloomy day, her heart was full of excitement in anticipation of opening the envelope. She recognized the logo on it and smiled.

She lived on her own. Her sight wandered toward the large picture of two young boys on the main wall. One of them held a soccer ball, and the other had a baseball bat. She looked at the painting with pride. "My twins," she whispered.

It hadn't been easy to raise two boys alone, but somehow she managed. However, her boys were grown and living their own lives. When her sons left home, loneliness began to creep into her soul, like a silent malady. Only her job running her bookstore and writing gave her solace. She never wanted to move away from Strathmore, her quaint little town. It was her home.

Christine gazed at the envelope in her hand and put it down on a side table. She decided to open it later because she wanted to delay the thrill of it, like a child licking the remains of an ice-cream cone unrushed.

She recalled how everything started. About six months ago, she received a phone call from her cousin, Liza, from Calgary, who said she was worried about their uncle Michael.

"What's wrong with him?" Christine asked.

"He's in deep trouble."

"Why?"

"He is in prison," Liza said.

Christine gasped. "What?"

"I'm not sure of the details, but I think he got involved with the wrong people and it turned out poorly. That's all I know."

"I'm sorry for what he's going through."

"Yeah, I feel the same way."

"Where is he?" Christine asked.

"Drumheller. That's why I'm calling. You don't live far from there. Maybe you could visit him."

"Sure. Poor uncle, I feel for him."

" So do I. OK, Chris, give him my best when you see him."

"Yes, I will."

From her childhood, Christine had fond memories of her uncle, and now that his life had taken this turn, she considered it her moral duty to visit him.

The next day, Christine drove to Drumheller, about ninety kilometers from Strathmore. As she arranged her woolen scarf, the winter breeze made her shiver. She entered the main office and signed the visitors' register. A female officer asked Christine to follow her to the inspection room. She had to empty her purse and allow the officer to pat her down from head to toe.

Once she passed the inspection, she was directed to the visitors' area.

Her uncle was delighted to have a visit. She'd have liked to hug him, but they only could talk over the phone through a thick window.

"Hello, Christine. So nice of you to visit," the old man said.

His tired aspect and faint smile touched Christine's heart. She remembered him as a tall person, taking her in his strong arms and twirling her around as she pretended to be an airplane.

"Hello, Uncle. How are you feeling?"

"Not too bad, dear. My asthma gets me at times. Besides that I'm OK, I guess."

"I brought you some blueberry muffins. Your favorite

kind, if I recall correctly and I also have a couple of books. The guard is going to give them to you later."

"Thank you."

On impulse, she asked, "Uncle, why are you here?"

"My dear child, I've made some bad choices and I'm deeply sorry." His eyes overflowed with guilt. "But, please, spare me the embarrassment of going into details."

"I understand. Sorry to make you feel uncomfortable."

When the visit was over, she stood by the reception counter to sign her exit. On the prison's bulletin board, she read a notice asking for volunteers interested in exchanging correspondence with inmates. Without much thought, she decided to join the program and wrote her name beside one empty slot.

What an awful place, full of lonely people, paying their debt to society. I'm glad I can help, she thought as she left the building.

* * *

Christine had almost forgotten about her commitment to writing when she received the first letter. It read:

Dear Ms. Wallace,

I appreciate you taking the time to put your name down to participate in this program. I'm glad to have someone to write to. I consider it pertinent to explain to you why I'm serving time. I was charged with criminal negligence causing death ....

At that point, Christine stopped reading and sighed. The words 'criminal' and 'death' made her uncomfortable. Did she do the right thing signing up for the prison's correspondence program? Her bookstore and her writing kept her busy. Also, she had a few good friends she hung around with. Wasn't that enough? She shook her head and continued reading.

I want to be honest with you and explain the events that brought me here. It was a Friday night at the local pub. A guy tried to get fresh with a young girl, but she refused his advances. He kissed her forcibly, anyway. I'd had a few drinks, and I wasn't thinking straight. I grabbed the guy by the neck, dragged him to the street, and punched him hard. He hit his head on the pavement. The police arrived and the paramedics took him

to the hospital. He died two days later of a brain hemorrhage and I was charged. I've been here for two years.

After knowing my story, if you decide not to write, I'll understand.

Sincerely,

Matthew Gibson

. . .

After reading Matthew's letter, a wave of empathy washed over her. *Poor man. If one of my sons was ever in a similar situation, I hope someone would show them compassion*, she thought.

She wrote back.

Dear Mr. Gibson,

I hope my letter brings you company in the difficult times you are going through. Don't be too concerned. After reading your story, I feel comfortable keeping up with our correspondence.

Please call me Christine. May I call you Matthew?

Dear Christine,

Thank you for your kind words. Let me tell you a bit about myself. I'm fifty and originally from England. I have lived in Calgary for the last twelve years, and I don't have any family in Canada. I spent my childhood in Liverpool. My mother was a school- teacher and my father was a mechanic. I never got along with him, because of his drinking problem.

When I turned eighteen I moved away to Manchester. I put myself through school, got an apprenticeship, and became an electrician. Being a skilled worker, it wasn't hard to emigrate to Canada. A decision I had never regretted...

. . .

Christine and Matthew kept writing to each other.

Dear Matthew,

I guess it's my turn to tell you about myself. I own a small book store and I have two great boys. Well, I shouldn't call them boys anymore. They are a couple of terrific men who brighten my life.

I'm writing a novel, and I'm happy to share with you this new adventure...

In the beginning, those letters were almost a commitment for Christine. A good thing to do for a lonely person. But after a couple of weeks, their writing became more personal. They were content to talk about their dreams and hopes through their letters. Their lives took a turn for the better as they found in each other affection and understanding.

It was Matthew who, in one of his letters, suggested she visit him. She was delighted to accept his request.

* * *

One morning, her cousin called to ask about their uncle Michael. Christine took the opportunity to tell her about Matthew.

"You have to be kidding me! I can't believe you have a

thing going with that guy. He is in jail, for God's sake," Liza said.

"I have someone who cares about me. Can you be on my side and wish me luck?"

"I do care about you. That's why I want to warn you. People don't change. If he committed a crime once, he probably could do it again."

"You don't know a thing about him. That's enough Liz. I don't want to keep talking. Goodbye." She hung up.

Christine decided that Liza's prejudiced attitude wouldn't overshadow her excitement about meeting Matthew. At last.

* * *

The anticipation of their first meeting filled Christine with joy. She wore her favorite dress, had her hair done, and put on makeup. It felt so good to spend some extra time on her appearance. When she got to the prison her heart was throbbing.

As she approached the visiting area, she recognized his features from a photograph she had. *Finally, that's Matthew*, she thought. The man who sat across from her had short blond hair and a freshly shaven face. She read a deep sadness in his big blue eyes. The pain of being deprived of his freedom, but at the same time, she found curiosity and hope.

She picked up the receiver and gazed at him through the plexiglass.

"Hello, Matthew."

"Hello, Christine." He cleared his throat. "I'm so happy to meet you in person."

"I'm glad I'm here," she said.

"Thank you for your letters. They mean so much to me," he said with an emotion-rich voice. His genuine smile lit up his face.

"I enjoy yours too."

For the rest of the meeting, they talked about Christine's sons, her store, and their common interest in books. She promised to bring him some soon.

Before she left, Matthew asked her to take a selfie of them. Getting the picture through the glass wasn't easy but she did it and promised him she'd bring him a copy on her next visit.

She kept writing her letters regularly and also visited him whenever she could.

After some time, their writing became more intimate. She couldn't remember the last time she'd experienced a warm feeling that enveloped her heart. It had been so long since anyone had said to her the things Matthew wrote in his letters:

My dear Christine:

Last night I was awake for hours, thinking today your letter was due.

I was right. As always your letters arrive just on time to give me solace, peace, and happiness when I need them most. They keep me going, allowing me to dream, and hope.

Indeed, my dearest, you give me a reason to live. Your letters are like a bright ray of sun warming up my solitary life.

I'm excited about the future because of you.

Christine smiled. She felt joyful about Matthew's presence in her life. When she phoned her children about having someone special she was interested in, they said they were happy for her and wished her the best.

She didn't mention Matthew was incarcerated. She wouldn't talk about it over the phone. There'd be plenty of time to explain the situation.

* * *

She waited for his letters with anticipation. In his last letter, he'd written:

My Christine,

I'm so happy to let you know my parole is coming soon. In my next letter, I'll tell you the exact date. My release would mean we could see each other without the constriction of the prison...

. . .

She picked up his most recent letter and decided she couldn't wait any longer to read it. With quivering hands, she opened the envelope. As she unfolded the letter, she noticed it was typed. Matthew's letters were handwritten. *How bizarre*, she thought.

It read:

Dear Ms. Wallace:

I'm afraid I'm not a bearer of good news. I regret to inform you that Mr. Gibson passed away last night in his sleep. The preliminary coroner's report stated the cause of death as a massive heart attack.

I was aware of your correspondence and visits to Mr. Gibson. I want to thank you for giving your time so generously to a person in need.

I'm very sorry for your loss.

Yours truly,

Samuel Lawrence

Chaplain

The Drumheller Institution,

Correctional Service of Canada.

A photo tumbled out of the envelope. Matthew's copy of the selfie she took, the one he kept on the wall of his cell. She ran her fingers over his features, remembering their last meeting and her feelings of joy, now shattered.

. . .

Christine walked to the window. It had started to rain, and droplets splattered the glass. Slow tears rolled down her cheeks and pain filled every crevice of her soul.

She held the letter close to her heart.

"Too late for us ...yeah, it was too late for us."

PINCOYA

After a hard day at sea, Juan dragged his fishnet to the beach and emptied its contents into a large bin. Some of the fish jumped and wiggled; others didn't. The sea had been generous, his net abounded with medium-sized and large species, enough to sell at the fish market and take home.

He wouldn't tell anyone about why his catch was bountiful. He'd prefer to die before revealing it to any living soul. His secret filled his heart with joy.

Ercilia, his mother would be happy to see that day by day he was getting better at his trade. He belonged to a family of fishermen and now at seventeen, he no longer considered himself a novice.

The small island lived on what the sea offered, a variety of fish, mollusks and seaweed. Their livelihood depended on how the sea behaved. It had been like that for centuries.

His mother was always concerned about his well-being. "The sea is treacherous, son. Never trust calm waters. The wind may change, the storm will rage and you'll be lucky to survive. It is then when Pincoya comes to the surface," she said.

Since he was a child, Juan's mother had talked about Pincoya. "She is an ethereal being, like a sea fairy. People believe she is half woman, half fish, and lives in the water." That's all she said.

But Juan had heard other versions. Pincoya was in love and betrothed to a strong, good-hearted fisherman. But the sea, always hazardous during a stormy day, took him away. She thought she would die the same day her lover did. It didn't happen.

Her life became a misery. She cried every day by the seaside, and her tears caused the ocean to rise and overflow its banks. Her sobs augmented the winds, giving birth to strong storms that made fishing almost impossible.

The islanders became hostile. They ostracized her, blaming her for their poor fishing. How would they feed their families? People thought she was bewitched by an evil spirit.

She tried to ignore what was happening, but the gossip weighed too heavily on her heart. She had to do something. And she did.

One moonless night, she walked into the sea to find her lover.

It was then that the legend of Pincoya was born.

But the truth was quite different. Only a few privileged elders were aware of the veracity of Pincoya's beginnings.

* * *

Zulema, Juan's grandmother, sipped her tea with trembling hands. She was almost blind, but she didn't need her sight to perceive Juan had arrived. Her keen sense of smell told her the boy had opened the door to her cabin. His scent mimicked the sea. Joy permeated her old heart when she inhaled her grandchild's essence.

"Is that you, my angel?" She always called him that, because when he was born, she glimpsed around the baby's head a halo illuminating his tiny face.

No one else saw it.

"You know it's me, *Mamita.*" Juan kissed her forehead.

"Sit by my side, close to the fire," she said. Holding a long stick, she shuffled the embers of the brazier. "How's school going?"

"Fine, but boring. I prefer to fish or walk by the seaside. It gives me joy. There is a magic about the sea and I feel drawn to it."

"Be careful. Once the sea casts its spell on you, it will hold you in its net of wonder forever."

"*Mamita,* what do you know about Pincoya? I've heard different stories. Tell me the real one. I'm curious."

"I love stories, my angel. I'll tell it to you, the same way my mother told me."

* * *

Everything started the day Pincoya was born. Consuelo, Pincoya's mother, kissed her baby's forehead and laid her down on a basket by the seaside. As she waded out to her boat, she eyed dark clouds menacing the sky. *I'll be fine*, she thought, *it won't take me long to get a few fish.*

But after a short while, a sudden storm ruthlessly whipped the skies. Ferocious wind and relentless rain made it impossible for Consuelo to control her fishing boat, which rocked side to side with the swaying of the waves, like an autumn leaf under a swift breeze.

Teeth chattering and heart thumping in her chest, Consuelo thought of her baby girl. She wanted to shout her name, even if it meant expending the last of her energy. She fought with all her might against the strength of the waves. But the wrath of the sea triumphed. She lost her boat, but saved her life.

Crawling along the sand she found her way to where she'd left Pincoya's basket. It wasn't there.

For a moment her heart stopped and she couldn't breathe. When she was able to, she knew immediately her next step.

She walked into the sea to look for her baby. As her body submerged, she loved the serene brutality of the ocean with each breath of wet, briny air.

. . .

At this point in the narration, Juan's eyes were fixed on his grandmother's face, as he listened with his heart.

She kept going.

The darkness of the ocean's depths impressed Consuelo at first. She squinted trying to distinguish her surroundings. She preferred to close her eyes. A magical world, mysterious and dark appeared under her lids. Beautiful starfishes in iridescent colors clung to rocks, giant manta rays flew like butterflies, and luminous fishes danced around.

But amid all this beauty, she couldn't find Pincoya.

Until she did.

Consuelo realized she had roamed the waters for years looking for her daughter, because when she saw her, Pincoya had grown into a beautiful young girl. No words were needed. The mother and daughter embraced, jubilant that the pain of their separation was over and that they would be together for eternity. Joy wrapped them in a protective mantle.

But the legend didn't end there. People said that all the fishermen who died at sea would live again in the depths of the ocean. An eternal, happy life without pain, without sorrow, waiting for their loved ones to join them one day in the ocean's depths.

When she finished the story, Zulema warmed her hands close to the brazier and gently rubbed her face. Juan looked at her earnestly. "*Mamita*, do you truly believe this story?"

"I certainly do, my angel." She caressed the boy's head. "When my time comes, I'll join them. I want my body to be left by the seaside. Promise me, you'll do that."

"I promise, *Mamita.*"

She smiled gently. Her knotted fingers swayed as she spoke. "When the tide rises I want to dance with the waves, move with the sea, let the rhythm of the water take me away."

He listened to the old woman in awe. It seemed like she was reading his mind, saying the words hidden in his heart since he'd met Pincoya.

No one knew why Juan disappeared for hours and when he found his way home, Ercilia asked, "What happened to you, my boy? There's a strange gleam in your eyes."

He kept silent, and a shy smile appeared on his face. He hugged his mother tenderly and left. His secret meetings with Pincoya permeated his young heart with indescribable joy.

It was another good day at sea. Juan's nets were full of fish. He left them at the beach, got on his boat, and set out to the deep water where his love, Pincoya, waited for him.

AND THEN, THERE WAS LIGHT

Allison fumbled around the nightstand for her bell, but instead, she spilled the glass with what remained of her whisky. The vein in her forehead throbbed and her rage built up to a scream, "Mariana, where the hell are you?"

She wiggled on her four-poster bed, her back resting against the velvet headboard.

Her enraged distorted features couldn't hide her beauty, despite the two-inch scar on her right temple that extended to her hairline. The scar was barely noticeable but Allison could not see it anyway. Life had abandoned her eyes.

The girl knocked at the bedroom door. She wore a maid's uniform, too large for her frame. A thick black braid hung to the small of her back. Her dark-brown skin, short stature and small eyes gave away her Indigenous heritage.

"*Buenos dias,* Miss Allison. You called?"

"Are you deaf? I've been calling forever, shouting for you. Where is my frigging bell?"

"*Perdon,* Miss Allison," Mariana said and placed the chrome bell on the extended hand.

" I've told you a thousand times to leave the bell on the right side of my lamp."

"But, I did."

"Be quiet. Don't interrupt me. Look what you made me do, I think I spilled my glass. It's your fault for not following my orders."

Mariana fixed her stare on the floor. "I'm sorry."

"The agency told me you spoke English well, but if you can't follow instructions, you're of no use to me."

"Please, I need this job," she pleaded.

" Fine, you may stay. For now. Bring my breakfast."

Mariana entered the kitchen in tears. She didn't like her job as Allison's housemaid, but the agency offered her the only available position. She joined John, the gardener and Elsa, the cook.

"What's wrong?" Elsa touched the girl's shoulder.

"She's so mean. She hates me," Mariana said.

Elsa shook her head. "No, she doesn't. She hates her life, I pity her, having so much money and being so unhappy."

John, who was listening, interrupted their dialogue. " How'd you feel if you couldn't see? She wasn't born blind, as you know, which makes things even worse. Don't you think so?"

"I do feel sorry for her, but she isn't a nice person. I wish I could leave, but I can't," Mariana said as she prepared the breakfast tray.

Back in her bedroom, Allison grabbed her cane and took a few steps, contemplating her dilemma. She needed to find a solution to her problem. Dr. Harris said he could perform the surgery, but the outcome would be uncertain because it was experimental. Allison was willing to do whatever it took to regain her sight.

In the beginning, the doctor wasn't convinced about doing the procedure, but Allison had a hidden strategy. He had a mistress and a child outside of his marriage. If he didn't agree to Allison's request, she'd expose him to his wife.

Mariana's voice startled her. "Your breakfast is ready."

"Is my tray set as I ordered?"

"*Si*, Miss Allison. Orange juice and water on the right side, your coffee at the center, and your toast on the left side."

"Fine. You may leave now."

* * *

Hunched over the laundry room sink, Mariana hand-washed Allison's silk blouses. Doing her task mechanically, she thought of her family and her quaint little mountain town, in her native country: Guatemala. Leaving them wasn't easy, but since her father passed, the family could hardly survive. Putting food on the table was a daily struggle.

On top of that, her son, Eduardo, a scrawny but handsome five-year-old boy, needed surgery the family couldn't afford. Mariana's determination to work hard to save money was the reason she tolerated Allison's acerbic remarks.

Mariana's aunt Claudia had been living in Miami for several years. The girl wrote to her, asking for help. After a few months, Mariana obtained a working visa and landed a job as a housemaid for Allison, a forty-year-old blind woman.

Living in a large house felt unfamiliar to Mariana. The place was fancy and elegant but cold. Even though it was summertime, it was the ambience rather than the weather that made it so.

She wondered how someone could be sullen most of the time, having everything one needed. But soon she realized her unfairness. Being surrounded by darkness, deprived of the joy of looking up at the sky, seeing flowers bloom in spring, unable to enjoy the beauty all around. It was a tragic way of living.

The sound of Allison's bell brought Mariana back from her reverie. She ran upstairs, hoping her boss would keep her temper.

"Why did you take so long ?"

"*Perdon,* Miss Allison, but I was in the laundry room washing your blouses."

"I don't want to hear your excuses. Take me to the bathroom."

After Allison finished showering, the girl helped her get ready for her morning routine: lying on her favourite chaise and listening to music. A glass of whisky sat on the side table. She closed her eyes, allowing the music to permeate every crevice of her being. Soon, she dozed off.

A succession of images danced in front of her eyelids. She saw herself young, vibrant, and full of life running around her parents' manicured gardens, trying to catch her spoiled poodle.

The day she met Jack at that cozy bar where every Saturday a local group played jazz, came to her mind. He looked so handsome with his friendly smile and his fitted shirt, she could guess the contour of his strong muscles. He approached her, and they talked. They became good friends at first but later an irresistible attraction took over, and love flourished.

Six months later, they got married.

The images ran one after the other in rapid sequence. Allison remembered that day, her hair flapping in the wind, the sun gently on her face and Jack's child-like expression behind the wheel translated to one word: happiness.

Everything happened so quickly. The van coming in the opposite direction crossed the double yellow line and struck Jack's car head-on.

The world went black.

When she woke up in a hospital bed, a large bandage covered her head including part of her face. The doctors told her she had suffered traumatic optic neuropathy, a fancy way of saying she'd lost her vision.

Jack didn't survive his injuries.

* * *

Rays of sun filtered through the sitting room's clear curtains. As Mariana dusted the crystal figurines in the walnut cabinet, she heard the ring of the main entrance. Any other day she'd have waited for Elsa to answer the call, but not on Mondays when the mailman made his rounds. She sprinted downstairs, hoping to get a letter from home.

She got one.

Heart pounding with joy, she shoved the letter into her uniform pocket. She'll read it later. It was time for Allison's lunch.

In the kitchen, Elsa had the tray ready. Mariana checked it to make sure everything was placed in the right spot.

"Thanks. Wish me luck."

"Yeah, good luck. Let's hope she is in a good mood."

After Allison finished her lunch, she called Mariana. "Just leave the tray and sit." The girl bit her lower lip and sat on the edge of the chair. Allison turned her head toward the noise and asked, "How is your son doing?"

"He is very sick. I got a letter from my mother today but I haven't read it yet."

"Oh, I see. I need to ask you a question. How far are you willing to go to help your son?"

"I will do whatever it takes to help him." She sounded determined.

"Good. You need money for his surgery, don't you?"

She wrung her hands, "You know I do."

"You could have the money you need, but I must have something in return." Allison stood, grabbed her cane and walked toward Mariana.

"What would that be?" The girl's voice shook.

"Your vision."

Mariana gasped, and for a few seconds, she couldn't breathe. "I don't understand", she said when she could talk.

"I'm having eye surgery to restore my vision and I need a donor."

The girl gulped as she gathered the courage to ask, "You want to take my eyes?

"Well, not exactly, but yes, I need your ability to see. It's complicated but after the surgery, you'll be blind. You said you'd do anything to save your son's life, didn't you?"

Mariana felt like a lightning jolt had hit her; nausea swirled in her stomach. She took a deep breath. "Excuse me," she said and sprinted out of the room.

After Mariana left, Allison sat by her bed. She decided the girl needed time to think about the offer. It would benefit both: Mariana's son would get his surgery and Allison would get her donor.

It sounded terrible to condemn a young person to blindness. But horrible things happen every day, and people learn to put up with them. The same way she had endured in darkness. But not anymore.

Nighttime arrived, and Mariana couldn't sleep ruminating about Allison's proposal. What about if Eduardo could have his surgery and have a normal life? Even if she couldn't see, she could learn to read. She'd seen it in movies. She was aware blind people could have special dogs to help them to get around.

Maybe, just maybe, it wouldn't be too hard to adjust to a new way of living.

As the rose-pink light of dawn painted the sky, resolution and calm settled in her heart. She'd made up her mind.

* * *

The next morning Mariana entered Allison's bedroom carrying the breakfast tray.

"*Buenos dias.* When you are done, could I please talk to you?"

"About?"

"Your offer."

"Fine. I'll call you when I'm finished."

Mariana paced the corridor outside Allison's room. Her thoughts were in a whirl, and her heart thumped widely. She entered the room when Allison called her.

"Have a seat."

"Gracias. I prefer to stand," she said, even though her knees trembled.

"What do you want to tell me?"

Mariana inhaled deeply through her nose, then exhaled

through her mouth. She looked at Allison earnestly. "I accept your offer. I'll be your donor."

Before Allison could talk, the girl added, "Last night I read the letter my mother sent. My son's condition is getting worse. He doesn't have long to live without the surgery. I love my child and I'd give my life for him. So, trading my vision for his well-being is worth it."

As Mariana talked about her son's condition, something in Allison's heart threatened to shatter, but she dismissed the feeling.

"Very well. I'm happy you've accepted. We will talk more about it later. You may go now."

Allison grabbed her cane and walked to the open window. The pleasant warmth of the morning sun brushed her face. The fresh aroma of her rose garden filled the air. She pressed her lips together and her lifeless eyes welled.

In the following days, Allison went through her routines, but her mind couldn't stop going over her decision to move ahead with the surgery.

One morning, after Allison finished her breakfast, Mariana asked, "Miss Allison, I need to tell you something."

"What?"

"Today I got a letter from my mother. It's addressed to you." She took an envelope from her uniform pocket.

"That's bizarre," Allison said, frowning. "Fine. Read it to me."

With a quivering voice, the girl read;

. . .

"Dear Miss Allison,

Mariana told me about the agreement between you two. In the beginning, I was horrified by your request. I prayed and asked God for guidance. As always, he listened. I understand we should be thankful for what we have.

Because of you, I'll have my grandchild to keep loving. And for that, I'll be eternally grateful. Don't feel bad about my girl's blindness. It was her decision. When love guides our actions, peace settles in our hearts. I'll take care of my daughter until my last day. I'll be her eyes.

Yours

Luz Maria Canales

Mariana's mother."

A strange light glowed in Mariana's eyes, as she finished reading. She smiled.

Allison's voice quavered when she said."Please leave."

* * *

The following morning, when Mariana brought the breakfast tray, she noticed Allison's face looked different. Maybe a hint of confusion, resignation or compassion. She couldn't tell.

"*Buenos dias,* I have your tray," she said.

"Thanks, but I'm not hungry." Her voice sounded tired, defeated. "Take it back to the kitchen."

"You don't want to keep your juice?"

"No, I don't."

Mariana took the tray back, sat by the kitchen counter and sighed.

Elsa gave her a questioning look. "Something wrong with you?"

"I'm concerned about Miss Allison. She eats little and has refused her usual mid-morning whisky for a couple of days. That's not like her."

"Why do you care?"

"She is a human being. I care."

"Well, you shouldn't. She doesn't give a shit about us." Elsa clicked her tongue and left the kitchen.

Back in her room, Allison mulled over her thoughts. The letter from Mariana's mother touched her deeply. The woman was grateful her grandson would have a chance to live a normal life. She understood Mariana will lose her sight and then she asked Allison not to feel guilty about her grisly request. The woman's selflessness seemed impossible to comprehend.

For no apparent reason, the image of Jack came to her mind. Her heart ached. She rubbed the heel of her palm against her chest, wondering how life would have been if he were by her side– if the accident hadn't occurred– if she weren't blind. Too many -'ifs'- to think about.

But reality hit her in the face. Her blindness was much more than her inability to see. She realized she was blind to Mariana's pain.

. . .

Later on, preoccupation with Allison's well-being led Mariana to check on her boss. The girl knocked softly and poked her head through the open door. "Excuse me, I wonder if you need anything?"

"No, thanks. Please, come in."

When Mariana entered the room, Allison sat in her bed. Her eyes seemed swollen and sadder than ever, her mouth set in a fixed and uninviting line.

"We need to talk. Have a seat."

Mariana sat, hands crossed on her lap. She blinked rapidly.

"Did you read your mother's letter beforehand?"

"Of course not. That wouldn't be right, The letter was addressed to you."

A heavy silence settled between the two women. "Your mother is an extraordinary person."

The girl smiled widely. *"Si, Mama es fantastica."*

Allison closed her eyes and took a deep pained breath. "I've been thinking about my surgery," she said.

"Are you nervous about it?" Mariana asked with genuine concern.

"No, I'm not." She rubbed the back of her neck. "I've decided not to have the procedure."

Mariana listened, mouth agape with incredulity, but didn't dare to utter a word.

"Your mother's letter opened my eyes and showed me what I couldn't see, not because I'm blind but because I'm heartless." Tears threatened.

"You are not heartless. You're just sad and lonely."

"I don't want your pity. Just listen. I'll give you the money you for your son's surgery." She paused for a moment. "I know how it feels to lose someone you love. I don't want you to go through the same."

Mariana couldn't believe what she heard. "Are you sure?" she asked in a thin voice.

"Of course I'm sure. My decision is final."

"Oh, I don't know how to thank you." Tears blurred Mariana's vision.

Allison's voice cracked and she cleared her throat."That's fine. Please, leave. I need some time by myself."

After the girl left the room, Allison grabbed her cane and walked toward the warmth radiating from the open window. She closed her eyes, but behind her lids, there was light.

THE MARK

Cloudy skies threatened a rainy day; a chilly breeze crept in through the open window of the small apartment. Louise tried to close it tight, but couldn't. She wrenched on the window frame, but it was stuck. It had been broken for over a month. The walls needed to be repainted, and the old carpet was stained all the way through.

"Shit. Everything is falling apart in this place." She had complained to the landlord to no avail.

She rubbed her naked arms to warm them up, walked to the bathroom, and looked at the image in the cabinet mirror. Putting up her long blond hair, she ran her index finger along the mark across her ivory neck. A deep purple discoloration on the side of it had turned bluish. She grabbed a silk scarf sitting on a chair and wrapped it around her neck to hide the mark.

Every time she scanned her crummy place, a feeling of disappointment came over her. Her phone beeped and a message from Kristina, her older sister, illuminated the screen. "I'm here."

Louise rushed out of the apartment, locked the door, and made her way to the street.

* * *

Kristina saw her sister running toward the car; her light skirt and silk scarf flapping with her brisk movements gave her the appearance of a winged being. She stared at Louise's slim figure with admiration and a hint of envy. But above all, she loved her sister.

"Sure took you a bit longer," Kristina said.

"Sorry to make you wait, sis."

"No worries, but we have to hurry up. We shouldn't be late for your appointment."

While driving, Kristina scanned the neighborhood. "This place looks kind of rundown."

"Are you planning to move to a nicer area?"

"We'll move when we can afford something better. This is just temporary."

"I see."

While Kristina drove, Louise's mind recalled the tragedy that changed their lives forever.

On January 20, her birthday, their parents decided to

surprise her with a visit and they set out from Toronto to her home in Montreal.

On the way, a drunk driver appeared out of nowhere and crashed into their car, killing them both. The unfairness of the situation broke the sisters' hearts. Their beloved parents, soft-spoken school teachers, were taken from them just a year after their retirement.

Louise was aware Kristina tried to cope with her loss the best she could. But her sister became bitter, upset with herself and the rest of the world. She criticized every aspect of Louise's life, from the second-hand clothes she wore to the people she dated.

She remembered the way Kristina was before the accident: vivacious and outgoing, but temperamental at times. Despite her mood swings, Louise never doubted her sister loved her.

After the death of their parents, a deep sadness, like a dark sky before a storm, wrapped Kristina's heart.

But Louise's condition was worse. She felt guilty and couldn't stop asking herself what if her parents had decided to stay home rather than visit her? What if she'd lived in Toronto instead of Montreal?

It was all her fault.

Depression took residence in Louise's soul. She couldn't eat or sleep and she forgot about personal hygiene. She had to quit her nursing studies.

A good friend pushed her to ask for help. She did.

* * *

Louise walked into the facility. A sign in golden letters read Dr. Barney Jackson, Psychiatrist. She steadied herself and took a deep breath. She had seen the doctor before, and after the initial visit, he recommended she should spend time at his inpatient clinic to be further assessed.

Louise met Ivan on her admission day. He wore his straight blond hair in a ponytail, a well-kept mustache over his upper lip. His name tag read Ivan, Care Aide.

During her stay at the clinic, they saw each other occasionally and chatted a few times, but nothing too personal. She sensed though, he was attracted to her. The day before her discharge, he asked her if he could get in touch when she went home. She gave him her phone number. They became close friends and he told her his story.

His family emigrated to Canada from Russia when he was six years old. His father earned a living as a construction worker, while his mother stayed home looking after three children under ten. His father, a violent man, unable to control his rage, used to beat his wife and children. After each incident, the father would feel overwhelmed with remorse, cry, and ask for forgiveness.

Ivan's sad life story deeply touched Louise. It was so different from hers. She grew up with caring and loving parents, never witnessing any roughness between them. She remembered her childhood as a haven of peace, a place of shelter and protection.

But Ivan grew up experiencing violence. That's all he knew.

Falling in love with him came easily. He needed a woman to give him some tenderness and she was ready to offer it. After her parents died, Louise felt like a child in an abandoned tunnel, lost, lonely, and cold. She dreamt about making Ivan part of her solitary life.

In the beginning, being together was fantastic. Walking to the nearby park, going to the movies, and cooking nice meals filled them with happiness.

The first argument had to do with a misunderstanding at a social gathering. Louise talked and laughed with an old friend she hadn't seen in years. When they got home, they had a heated discussion because Ivan thought she had flirted with her friend in front of everybody. He lost his cool and slapped her. He immediately was remorseful and asked for forgiveness. He even cried.

She forgave him.

The next time, she went out with friends and came home late. He was furious and smacked her again. It took him a few hours to ask for forgiveness once more, but he did.

The last episode was the worst. He grabbed her by the neck. It left a mark. But she couldn't pardon him this time. Resentment started to grow in her heart.

* * *

Even though she had seen the doctor before, she always was uneasy talking about her feelings. As he entered the room, she bit her lower lip.

"It's good to see you again Louise. How are you feeling today?"

She looked at the floor. "A bit blue, as usual."

"If you want to, you could lie down on the sofa."

She did.

He grabbed a chair and sat facing her. He observed the girl with empathy. "Sometimes sharing traumatic experiences with others who went through similar situations is beneficial. I have a proposition for you. Do you think group therapy could help you somehow?"

She looked at the ceiling. "To be honest, I don't know."

"I'm pretty sure it will help," he said.

"Are you taking your meds?"

"Yep, every day."

"Louise, you need to understand you're not responsible for your parents' accident. In life, terrible things occur, and there isn't much we can do about them."

He paused for a moment. "The accident happened almost a year ago. How do you feel about it now?"

She crossed her arms in front of her chest, without answering.

"Talk to me, please."

"What do you want me to say? I'm always sad. I feel lonely, even with people around me. Sometimes I think I'd be better off dead."

The doctor gazed at her, his blue eyes pleading. "Let me help you, Louise."

She kept silent.

"Do you live on your own?"

"No. I live with Ivan, my partner."

"I'd like to get in touch with him"

Her hair lifted on her nape and arms. "No, please, don't." Her voice quivered.

Dr. Jackson's brow furrowed. "Why not?"

"I have my reasons and I don't want to talk about it. You could get in touch with my sister if you want."

A questioning look appeared on the doctor's face. "That's fine. I'll speak to Kristina instead."

They talked for another half an hour, but to Louise, those were empty words. Nothing more. In her mind, she'd already found a way to break free from her misery.

The doctor stood from his chair. "Is there anything else you'd like to tell me?"

"No, I don't think so."

"I need to see you again soon. Could we talk tomorrow? My receptionist will give you the appointment. In the meantime, you have my number, right? Please, phone me anytime, okay?"

"I will. Thanks," she said and left the room.

* * *

Louise rushed to her sister's car parked a couple of blocks from the medical building. A knock on the window car startled Kristina."Shit, you scared me!"

"Sorry, sis."

"How was your appointment? Was Dr. Jackson helpful?"

"Yeah, I guess. He said I have to keep taking my meds and see him tomorrow. He said he

needs to talk to you. He'll phone you."

Kristina's concerned look was written all over her face. "Sure, I'll wait for his call."

During the ride back to Louise's, Kristina eyed her sister frequently. "I care about what happens to you," she said. "I want you to be happy. You look so sad. Is Ivan good to you, Lou?"

Louise's sorrowful eyes didn't meet her sister's. Instead, she touched Kristina's hand. "Don't worry about me, sis. I'll figure things out."

When they arrived at their destination, Kristina parked. Before her sister got out she said, "You call if you need anything. Promise me."

"I promise."

"If I don't hear from you tonight, I'm going to call to see how you're doing."

"That's fine."

Louise got to her apartment and walked into the kitchen to get a hot drink. Holding the warm cup of tea between her cold fingers, she looked around the small, crowded place, sat on the worn-out sofa, closed her eyes, and immersed herself in thought.

She never imagined things could turn out the way they had. When Ivan got enraged, he couldn't control his actions. He tried to strangle her once; he might do it again. She was tired of living with him.

Or maybe she was tired of living. Period.

Her state of mind darkened her thinking. She put the cup in the kitchen sink, got her phone and messaged Ivan.

She tugged on a strand of hair as she typed. "Hi, how are you?"

"What do you want?"

"I was just thinking about you." She swallowed, worried she annoyed him. "Are you working a long or short shift tonight?"

"Short."

"Oh. I just wondered." His abrupt answer did nothing to ease her discomfort.

"Stop bugging me at work. Unlike you, I have a job to do." His harsh words stabbed at her heart.

Great, now she'd pissed him off again. She cringed knowing she'd pay for that later.

She tried to be strong, but couldn't. Dabbing her tears, she sat on the couch. Time seemed to stand still.

* * *

Ivan arrived at their building and parked the car, slamming the door with such force, its sound resonated through the parkade.

A noise at the door interrupted Louise's thoughts. "Ivan, is that you?"

"Of course, it's me. Who else lives here?"

She didn't reply. "Did you have a good day?"

"I had a crappy one. I hate my job." He threw his knapsack on the floor.

"I'm tired and hungry." He opened the fridge. "This shit is almost empty!" He banged its door.

She scissored her bottom lip between her front teeth and bit down.

"Please, don't get angry." She jerked upright from her seat. A throbbing pain pressed behind her eyes.

"Sorry, I had to see Dr. Jackson today. I didn't have time to get groceries, but I'll make you a sandwich." Her voice shook.

"I don't want your fucking sandwich!" He slapped her face hard and her head jerked back.

She couldn't take it anymore. Her breathing grew heavier, she balled her hands into fists and confronted him. "You are an evil man. I hate you!"

She ran out of the room sobbing, got to the bedroom, slammed the door, and with trembling hands, turned the lock. Her pulse pounded in her ears. She stopped to catch her breath, went to the chest of drawers, and grabbed the gun.

She stood facing the door, hands behind her back, holding the weapon. "I'm glad my father taught me to shoot."

An enraged Ivan managed to kick open the door. He stomped into the room, his eyes reddened with anger.

"I'll kill you, bitch, I'll kill you!"

He saw her, facing him. In her right hand, pointed at his head, she held the gun.

His jaw dropped. His pupils dilated. "What are you doing?"

Louise put the pistol under her chin and pulled the trigger.

On the bedside table, her phone beeped, but no one answered.

UNDER A SPELL

How could I ever forget that summer? I was a fourteen-year-old girl who didn't have any friends and hated teachers. Being an only child made things worse. I was lonely and bored most of the time.

In 1923, my Father, Joao Cursino, was elected mayor of Sao Jose Dos Campos, a small town located in the Paraiba Valley, between Sao Paulo and Rio de Janeiro. We moved into the colonial residence, a majestic structure with thick adobe walls displaying huge paintings. There was a sitting room with a large piano, several bedrooms, a library, and a huge kitchen. In the main garden, beautifully manicured lawns surrounded a water fountain.

It was indeed a large place for a small family—my father, Joao, my father's second wife, Alanza, and me, Eloa. I was named after my mother, who died when I was born. We also had several servants who lived in separate quarters.

. . .

I remember how lonesome my father was after my mother died. He cried all the time, and he paced the gardens, thinking I didn't notice. But I did.

A year passed, and he met Alanza at a social gathering. She took advantage of my father's loneliness, and after a short courtship, they married. That was the worst day of my life; my world was turned upside down. Alanza and I didn't get along. She came into our home thinking she was a queen and the house was her castle.

She decided to change the whole residence to her liking by getting rid of everything Father and I treasured. She got new furniture, chandeliers, paintings, and curtains. The whole lot.

Alanza tried to erase Mother's memory. Not a chance. Everybody remembered her being kind to every person—servants, members of our congregation, family, neighbors—everyone.

I thought Alanza practiced witchcraft. I believed she cast a spell on Father, or something like that because, at times, I overheard strange noises coming from their bedroom—moans and murmurs. I thought for sure he was in trouble.

In my father's presence, she pretended to be kind to me and good to the servants. But when he left, her true self emerged. Malevolence, spite, and hostility were her main characteristics.

I couldn't stand her anymore. I had to do something. But what?

* * *

"Eloa, come here, please."

"Yes, Mother." (She made me call her that)

Alanza towered over me. Her skin, hair, and eyes were all the same golden brown, and her long curls cascaded down her shoulders. A velvety dress accentuated her figure. She looked like an angel, but her appearance was a facade. Malice reigned in her heart.

"I'm very disappointed in you, little lady."

"What did I do this time, Mother?"

"I talked to your teachers. They are not happy with you."

"You're late for classes, you don't do your homework, and your behavior is less than acceptable."

"That's all you wanted to tell me? May I be excused?"

"Don't be disrespectful. Is there anything you want to say in your defense?"

"My defense? I didn't know I was on trial."

"There's no point in talking to you. You are a brat. I'll tell your father about this

when he is back from Sao Paulo." The vein in her forehead throbbed along with the increasing tension in her voice.

"Do what you want, I don't care."

Rage distorted Alanza's face, and her jaw clenched. She whipped her hand back and slapped my face with such force, I fell to the floor. I stood, ran upstairs to my room and threw myself on the bed. An ocean of tears soaked my pillow.

From that day, I hated her even more.

The summer heat made me tired and grumpy. Every time I had the chance, I sneaked out to a nearby creek. It wasn't too big, but large enough to submerge myself in its lovely cool water.

During those times, I daydreamed about having a mother by my side. A real one, not an evil woman like Alanza. But that was only a dream. Mother was in heaven. I should accept my reality.

After Father, there was a person I truly loved—my Zenaida. She had taken care of Mother from an early age, and she had been by my side since the day I came into this world. I didn't think of her as a servant, I thought of her as a protector, a friend. When she hugged and squeezed me against her generous bosom, I was safe. Her skin was as dark as a moonless night, and her smile warmed the chill of dusk.

Zenaida had a hard life. Her parents had nine children and couldn't keep her, so they gave her to my grandmother, to work as a servant, at the age of twelve. After that, her family moved away and she never saw them again. She had lived with us since then. She never got married or had any children.

. . .

The next morning, I was still asleep when Zenaida entered my room.

"How is *minha menina* today?" she asked while she drew open the bedroom curtains. A big smile illuminated her lovely old face.

"Please, don't ask. I feel worse every day having that harpy around. You know

what she did yesterday?"

"No, *querida*. Tell me."

"You know Matheus the coachman, right?"

"Yes, I helped his mother bring him into the world. What about him?"

"Queen Alanza fired him and his family."

"Why?" Zenaida's hand flew to her chest.

"She said Matheus didn't keep the horses and the carriages the way she liked it and he'll have to leave with his wife and kids tomorrow. She does what she wants

because Father isn't here. I hate her."

"We shouldn't hate anyone, love. *Deus* will punish her when her time comes."

"Oh, Zenaida, God is not here to see what she does."

"God is everywhere, darling."

"My good Zenaida, you don't get it."

* * *

Through my upstairs window, I watched Alanza sitting on the main balcony, sipping her lemonade. In the distance, Father's white horse galloped toward the house. My heart thumped in my chest. But she remained sitting sipping her drink like she didn't care about a thing. I ran downstairs and waited at the bottom of the staircase.

Father dismounted and entered our residence. He gave his cape to the servant.

"*Bem- vindo,* my lord," the servant said, looking at his feet.

"Thanks, Alanyo."

Alanza left the balcony and stood at the main door, smiling. My father's large frame was imposing, and his dark brown hair reached the nape of his neck. His gray sideburns made him so handsome.

"Oh, *mi amor,* I've missed you." He held her tight against his chest and kissed her.

"I've missed you too, my love. Very much."

Father let Alanza go when he heard me shouting, "*Pai, Pai,* it's great to have you home!" I dashed into his arms and kissed him on both cheeks. "Oh my God, you are going gray."

His misty eyes looked down at me, "And you are a little lady already, my sweet girl."

After dinner, Father and Alanza retired to their bedroom and I went to my room. I waited a long while and sometime later, I crept to their door, pressing my ear to the keyhole.

"Love, we have to talk about something important," Alanza said.

"Do we have to now?" he asked, sounding half-awake.

"Yes, we do. It's about Eloa."

"What about her?"

"She isn't doing well at all. Doesn't like her governess and doesn't do her school work. I keep firing tutors, trying to find ones she may feel comfortable with, but it's no use. Eloa doesn't want to learn. She is unhappy. And she has been disrespectful to me."

"Darling, remember she is fourteen. You must have patience."

"It's not a matter of having patience. I do. You know I love her as my own. But we must think of what's best for her."

"And what would that be?"

"She should go to a proper school, where she could learn how to be a lady. A place where she could interact with girls her age. Don't you think?" Without waiting for an answer Alanza continued, "There is a prestigious Catholic school in Sao Paulo. Nuns run it. I have a friend whose daughter goes there. The child is quite happy."

"I don't like the idea of Eloa leaving home," Father replied.

"I don't like it either, but you want her to have a good education, don't you?"

"Of course, I do, but I need to talk to her first."

"Fine. You do that."

. . .

I tiptoed back to my room, overcome with distress. How could she be so mean? She wanted me to get away from my father. What had I ever done to her?

She was messing with the wrong girl. No doubt about that.

* * *

The next morning, when I entered the kitchen, Zenaida was peeling corn. I liked its smell, lush and fresh. She stood to greet me.

"How is *meu anjo* doing this morning?"

I hugged her and told her the bad news. My tears moistened her apron.

"Alanza wants to send me away to a nuns' boarding school. But I won't go. I prefer to die first."

"Don't say such things, my child."

I dried my tears with both hands. "Zenaida, I know your secret. I've known it for a long time."

"What do you mean?"

"I've seen you do weird, strange things, like the time you picked up that hummingbird with a broken wing. You ran your finger over the wound, and the bird flew away. If that's not magic, you tell me what it is."

A gentle smile illuminated Zenaida's old face. "I can't help myself, child. I was born with these powers. I don't want them, but they won't go away."

"Good. We'll need them to get even with Alanza."

"What are you talking about?"

"You heard me. I need your help to get rid of her."

"You don't know what you are saying."

"Yes, I do. Alanza is trying to convince Father to send me away, so I need her to disappear, to get sick, to become a cow, or to die. Whichever you choose. I don't care."

Zenaida gasped. "Oh, child. You are out of your mind." She looked at me square on. "I wouldn't use my powers to hurt anyone."

"Not even for me?" I asked.

Zenaida walked out of the kitchen and left me standing there.

Later that night, I put on the new necklace my father gave me. A knock on my bedroom door startled me.

"May I come in, *menina*?" he asked.

"Sure. Don't you think this necklace is gorgeous?" I kissed him on his cheek.

"You always look beautiful. Doesn't matter what you wear."

"Oh, *Pai*. You're so kind."

"Eloa, we need to talk."

An alarm sounded in my head at the tone of his voice. I realized the conversation would be a serious one.

"Alanza and I have been talking about your future."

I wrung my hands together. "What do you mean?"

"We want you to have a good education. How do you feel about going to boarding school?"

"I don't want to live away from you, *Pai.*" I blinked back tears.

"Eloa, you're old enough to understand life is all about learning to adjust."

I started to cry.

"Don't get upset, *menina.* We'll talk about it later."

* * *

A few months passed and Father didn't talk about sending me to boarding school again, which made me happy. But Alanza had changed. She looked tired, pale, and withdrawn. She didn't interact with the servants at all and had her meals in her rooms. At times I even heard her retching. Zenaida said she ate like a bird.

I had conflicting feelings. I kind of liked knowing Alanza wasn't doing well. That way, she'd leave me alone and stop insisting on boarding school. Maybe Zenaida gave her something to make her sick. I didn't know, and I was afraid to ask. But at the same time, I felt how Father looked so concerned about his wife's health.

One afternoon, a doctor came from Sao Paulo to see Alanza. After he left her room, Father escorted him to his carriage. When he came back, I noticed a strange expression on Father's face that I didn't know how to read.

As he went back to Alanza's room, he turned back to gaze at me. I tried to appear calm, but fear squeezed my heart.

Maybe his wife was dying.

. . .

In the following days, my preoccupation increased. I wondered about Alanza's condition—she looked sick, and I noticed dark circles under her eyes. I felt ashamed for wishing her ill.

After dinner, Father said to me, "Eloa, can we talk?"

My heart sank to the floor. I couldn't control my shaking knees. "I'm so sorry, Father!" Tears pooled in my eyes.

"What for?"

"For not being a good daughter."

"Don't say that. You're a great child."

I gave a deep sigh.

"Something special is going to happen to our family." A grin illuminated Father's handsome face.

"What is it, *Pai*?"

He smiled.

"I need you to be kind and understanding toward Alanza. Could you do that for me?"

"Sure *Pai,* but tell me what it is?"

"You'll find out soon, *menina*. For now, I need you to look after the house. I'm sure you and Zenaida will keep this place running smoothly until Alanza is well."

Without saying another word, he left me ruminating about what the future might bring.

In the end, things turned around for the better.

Father decided not to send me away to boarding school. He needed me around. Alanza's sickness turned out to be something unexpected.

A new family member arrived at our home! A little brother who changed my life forever.

How could I ever forget the summer of 1925?

ORDEAL IN AUTUMN

A warm summer breeze swayed the trees surrounding the village's plaza. The place seemed deserted; it was *siesta* time. Smoking a cigarette, two girls sat on a bench.

"I hope I can get out of this dull place, someday," said Mila. She inhaled her cigarette deeply and exhaled, making rings with the smoke.

"I'm lucky," her friend Susana replied. "As soon as I'm finished with school I'll be gone."

"How come?" Mila asked.

"My aunt got me a job as a receptionist, in the city," Susana squealed with joy.

"I'm happy for you, but I'll miss you," said Mila with a slack expression.

"Why don't you come with me?"

"Are you out of your mind? My father wouldn't allow it. He's too strict."

"Talk to him and if he doesn't approve, too bad. It's your life to live, is it not?"

Mila didn't answer but in her mind, the seed of self-determination had been planted.

Mila was born in Valle Maria, a small village about four hundred kilometers north of Buenos Aires. The area was mostly rural, and people earned a living from what they harvested. They raised cattle, worked in their dairy industry, grew wheat, and enjoyed a little bit tourism.

The oldest of three girls, Mila had to bear more responsibility than her siblings. Her parents Caterina, and Alberto, were hard-working people who governed their household rigorously. They loved their children, but their main concern was keeping up their farm.

Mila and her sisters were fed up with working the land. They had to get up early every day to feed the animals and then get ready for school. In the afternoon there were more chores to be done.

Summer was the worst, as the work increased. The whole family had to labor together in the fields. Crops needed harvesting, hay had to be gathered and ripe fruit picked to make jam and preserves. There was always a new task to perform.

. . .

On Sundays, the children were allowed to go to the river. "Hurry up, you two," Mila shouted to her sibling, as she donned her bathing suit. The girls grabbed their towels and ran to the door, pushing and shoving each other. They spent a glorious afternoon frolicking in the water like young ducklings.

If my plans turn out, I'm going to miss spending time with my sisters, Mila thought.

* * *

The next day, Mila painted her toenails, with her faithful chihuahua, Lupe, by her side. The dog stared at her with adoring eyes, as Caterina entered Mila's room.

"Hi, darling," she said and sat by her daughter's.

"Hi, there." Mila faced her. "Mama, I have something to tell you. When I finish high school, I want to go to Buenos Aires." She said it all in one breath.

Without concealing her surprise, Caterina asked, "to do what?"

"To look for a job. What else, Mom?"

"Your father won't let you go."

"I'll be eighteen by then, and I won't need his permission. We are in the twenty-first century, anyway, not the Dark Ages." She gave a sullen stare.

"Mila, what's wrong with you? Aren't you happy here?"

"Mom, this is the most boring place on earth! You are too old to get it."

"Love, be reasonable. Going to the city is a big step for a young girl to take."

"I'll be careful, I promise. You have to trust me, Mom. I won't disappoint you."

"I'm concerned about your safety, love."

"Mom, you know my friend Susana, right?"

"Sure."

"She'll have a good job in the city, working as a receptionist at her aunt's dental office. Susana said I could stay with her for a while. I'll be fine. Mom, give me a chance. I know you could convince Dad to accept my decision."

"I think this is a mistake, and I don't want you to go." Caterina touched Mila's hand. The girl flinched her away.

"Sorry, Mom, I've made up my mind. I'm going, anyway."

* * *

After a long day, Alberto finished working in the fields and went home. "I'm exhausted and starving," he said to Caterina.

"Wash your hands and I'll set the table." She smiled at her husband. They had been together for almost twenty years, but Caterina still saw him like the young man that played his guitar around the bonfire by the river bank, the day they met.

They ate and talked about their children and the work they had to do the next day.

Caterina cleared her throat. "Honey, we need to talk about Mila."

"What about her?" He finished his food.

"Mila has a project, and we should help her achieve it."

"What? Talk clearly and tell me what you mean." Tapping his fingers on the table, he grew impatient.

"When she finishes school, she wants to go to Buenos Aires."

"Now you're talking nonsense. She is a child. She should stay home and look for a job here."

"She isn't a child, she'll be eighteen soon."

Alberto banged on the table with his fist. "I'm the head of this family and I'll decide what Mila should do."

"Calm down, honey, let's talk things over," she said with a soothing voice. "She is almost an adult. We were nineteen when we got married."

He cracked his knuckles. "It's dangerous for a young girl to go to a big city alone."

"She'll stay with her friend Susana until she gets a job."

"So, you planned everything behind my back." His eyes protruded.

"No, you're mistaken. Mila told me about this yesterday. Please, honey, we should help her out," she pleaded.

After some persuading on Caterina's part, Alberto gave in.

* * *

A couple of months later, Mila was ready to leave. The fresh autumn morning chilled the air when Alberto and Caterina accompanied her to the bus station. They hugged their daughter and wished her good luck. Looking through the window, Mila reminisced about the good times she'd spent with her family, the afternoons by the river, the gathering for birthdays and celebrations; all was in the past now. She was eager to start her new life in Buenos Aires.

* * *

During her bus ride, Mila took in the city's vastness through her window. To her eyes, the scene looked impressive with its tall buildings, manicured gardens, and people swarming the streets. It'd take her some time to get used to the new place.

After a several weeks, Mila got a loft close to her work. One day, after meeting a few friends at Susana's place, Mila decided to walk to her studio, without realizing how late it was. She strode along the pitch-black street on a narrow sidewalk. The blanket of dry leaves crunched beneath her stride. Her hair danced in the breeze following the silent melody of the wind on that cold autumn night. She sensed someone was tracing her steps. She couldn't hear the stranger clearly, but she knew she was being followed.

A moonless night doesn't help at all, she thought. A panic settled in her mind the moment she realized the steps were getting closer. A shudder rippled down her body.

Suddenly, the stranger ran by her side, grabbed her purse,

and sprinted off. Heartbeat pounding in her ears, she caught her breath. Scared that the stranger may come back, she ran frantically to the middle of the street shouting for help.

Nobody was around.

Oh God, help me, help me, please, her mind kept repeating. Then she saw a taxi approaching the deserted street with a sign reading *LIBRE.* She stood in front of the car, waving her hands in the air, shouting, "Stop, stop!" The taxi halted just in front of her.

The cab driver unlocked the passenger door. Mila jumped into the car, adrenaline rushing through her veins. Her voice quivered when she talked to the driver. "Thank you, sir, for stopping. I was mugged, and someone grabbed my purse." She took a deep breath, "I was afraid he would come back or something."

The man didn't reply. Mila scrutinized his stare and didn't like what she saw. His piercing eyes scanned her pale face, and she trembled. He had a lustful gaze. Gritting her teeth, she dug her nails into her palms.

How can you be so stupid? A voice in her head said. *You should've stayed at Susana's place, instead of being here.* Mila ignored the voice and tried to compose herself. She said to the driver, "I'm going to *calle* Boedo, please." She added, "we are not too far".

The taxi driver didn't answer and kept driving. After a few minutes, he said, "I was going to my brother's place when you stopped me. It's his birthday. Why don't you come with me? It'd be fun."

"No, thanks but I can't. Please, take me home to *calle* Boedo."

"Come on. When we get there I know you'll like it." He grinned at Mila.

As the cab came to a stop at a red light, she opened the door, leapt out of the car, and ran away.

* * *

Caterina put two loaves of bread in the kitchen oven. She wore her gray hair in a bun at the nape of her neck. Deep wrinkles all over her face showed the hardship of country life.

She was exhausted after a hard day; it seemed like there were always too many things to do around the farm and not enough time to do them all. On top of farming, housework, cooking, and ironing, when night arrived and she lay beside Alberto, there was another duty to be performed.

After she heard her husband snoring, she quietly left the bed and went to the kitchen to make herself a hot drink. Sipping her tea, her mind wondered about Mila.

She hasn't called in over a week. That's not like her. Is she safe? She closed her eyes and prayed. Dawn lined the horizon in faint yellow shades when she returned to bed.

The next morning Caterina made breakfast and set the table for Alberto and the girls. She was slicing the loaf of bread she made the day before, as the morning news on the television started.

After the usual reports about wars around the globe, famine in Africa, and corrupt politicians all over South America, she wasn't interested in hearing anymore. But the television was in the kitchen, so she had little choice.

A journalist was saying, "Changing the tone, to some other news now. Last night another abduction occurred in Buenos Aires. A young female body was found in a scrap yard on the city's outskirts."

Caterina's heart fluttered. Her lungs refused to work. She turned her trembling head to look at the image the television portrayed. At that precise moment, the phone rang. Alberto answered it and when he heard who it was, he smiled and said, "Mila! It's about time!"

CIGARETTES AND TANGO

While driving to do the pick-up, Antonio recalled when Paulo gave him the jeep.

"You gotta have a car to make our deliveries, kid," he'd said.

Antonio gave a small shout. "Wow, thanks so much."

"Hold your horses, don't thank me. This is a loan. Not a gift."

Antonio parked the old jeep, at the usual place. Even though it dated back to the late fifties, now, almost twenty years later, it still performed well. He strode along the dark alley behind the Chinese restaurant. His heart thumped in his chest and its strength resonated through his brain. Pearly drops of sweat dripped down his young face. His dark eyes squinted, trying to adjust to the alley darkness make darker by the moonless night.

He was carrying a gun, a gift from his friend, Paulo.

"You better have this, kid. You never know when you are gonna need it."

Paulo had been friends with Antonio's father. When Antonio's father's passed after a lingering illness, Paulo became a father figure to him. After Antonio quit high school to look for work, he helped him get his first job at a hardware store.

He came back from his thoughts as a stray dog brushed his leg and ran off.

In the murky alley, as the minutes went by, Antonio kept pace. He gritted his teeth, let out a loud breath, and checked his watch once more. It was almost midnight.

This guy was supposed to be here an hour ago. Maybe he won't show up, he thought.

Just as Antonio was about to leave, a small-framed man, maybe in his forties walked toward him. Antonio had seen him before. Paulo called him Chino because of his Asian features and a peculiar cadence when he spoke.

"Sorry, I'm late, man," Chino said, "I had another delivery, and it went sour."

Antonio wasn't interested in small talk. "Don't waste my time. Did you bring my stuff?"

"Yeah, it's in my car."

Antonio didn't see any car. He frowned. "Where is it?"

"Beside that dumpster," Chino said, pointing to a big metal container.

"Okay, I'll bring the jeep around." Antonio parked the vehicle beside Chino's.

After the man gave him two large cardboard boxes, Antonio objected.

"Paulo told me you gotta give me three boxes," he said.

"I had to give a little present to the guys at customs. They always take a cut. Paulo is aware. That's the way this business works."

"OK, I'll take the boxes but I'm gonna check about it with Paulo later on."

Antonio put the boxes in the jeep and drove to Paulo's place.

Behind a large trash bin, a stranger observed the scene.

In the distance, an accordion played a tango. You could hear its melody anytime, anywhere in Buenos Aires.

* * *

Francisco Ramirez drank his coffee while checking his computer. A middle-aged man with a potbelly and bright eyes, he had spent over thirty years as a police officer. He was a respected member of the force.

Scratching his thinning white hair, he scrutinized pictures on his computer screen. It showed people of different ethnicities, young, old, male and female, known to the police. He paused when he found what he was looking for. A thin male with Asian features and a scar on his left cheek.

"I think this bird is gonna sing for me," he said as he enlarged the picture. Chino had been released from prison not long ago and Ramirez was certain he wouldn't be happy to go back.

The officer had been looking for the delinquents for a long time and was determined to get them even if it was the last thing he did before his retirement. As a widower without children, his work filled his life.

He knew the smugglers worked with a web of criminals amidst shanty towns and other impoverished areas. It was only a matter of time before he sent them to jail.

* * *

As Antonio entered Paulo's neighborhood, he couldn't fight a feeling of resentment. It seemed unfair that rich people had so much while so many had so little.

The huge houses looked imposing. Manicured lawns, well-kept gardens, and three or more fancy cars parked in the driveways completed the perfect picture of wealth.

I bet those houses have more than one bathroom. Maybe they have a pool. I'd love to rent Ma a house, even a humble one, he thought.

Paulo, a large man in his fifties, paced the garage floor and smoothed his mustache, in a monotonous mindless movement. He wore an expensive silk shirt and fancy leather shoes. His black eyes scanned the garage door.

After Antonio parked the jeep, Paulo said, "Hey, kid, you are late."

"Sorry, boss, Chino showed up almost at midnight."

"No sweat, kid. He called me already. Shit happens sometimes."

Antonio downloaded the two boxes into Paulo's van and asked," What is this stuff?"

"You don't wanna know."

"But ...but I do." His voice quavered.

"Well, I'll tell you because I trust you. But, you better keep your mouth shut, or you may be in deep shit. You got me?"

"I'm not stupid. I wouldn't tell anybody."

"Good. These are cigarettes."

"Just cigarettes?" Antonio's forehead wrinkled.

"Not your ordinary ones, moron. These are Americans, you know, Marlboro, Kent, Pall Mall, Camel."

"Uh, I see," Antonio said.

"This shit is great money, kid. It's good stuff, not like the crap we got here. Sometimes, if we are lucky, we could even get some whiskey. Corrupt politicians, high-ranking police officers, the filthy rich, you name it, they pay good money for this merchandise."

"But... is this legal?

"What are you asking?" The muscles in Paulo's neck strained.

"Ah ...nothing, boss." Antonio looked at the floor.

"You better never ask that again. For your own good. We have to give a little tip to the pigs at customs. But, that's all right because they let our shit come through the port. It's not a big crime, kid, and someone is gonna do it. It better be us."

Handing Antonio a roll of bills, Paulo told him, "This is your money for a job well done."

"Thanks, boss." He grabbed the wad of money and stuffed it in his pocket. He wanted to count it but didn't dare to do it in front of Paulo. When in the jeep by himself, he counted the bills: one thousand pesos! His jaw dropped.

In one delivery, he'd made twice the amount he earned working for a month at his hardware store job.

Wow, if this is how much smuggling pays, it's sure a good business, he reckoned.

* * *

Antonio's eyes sparkled and gleamed when driving the old jeep to his place. In his pocket, the wad of bills seemed to take a life of their own. He could swear his heartbeat was in those bills.

The boy and his family lived precarious lives. They didn't have enough money to rent a house on their own, so they paid for two rooms in a large place they shared with another family. Everyone shared the only bathroom.

A larger room was a kitchen, dining, and his mother's working space. The smaller room had a bed for Gloria, his mom, and a bunk bed for Antonio and his younger brother Bruno.

Since his father's death a couple years ago, Antonio felt responsible for his

family. His mother earned a living as a seamstress. She

owned an old sewing machine with a foot adapter: click, click, click. The sound had been Antonio and Bruno's constant childhood companion.

At that time, cars were rarely seen in the poor area where Antonio lived. He was proud to show the car to his mother.

"Ma, come out I want to show you something," he shouted, entering the main room.

A middle-aged woman emerged, drying her hands on her faded apron. Her premature wrinkles spoke of a hard life but they couldn't hide her beauty.

"What is this?" she asked looking, at the car and frowning.

"A car, Ma, what else?"

"I see that, but where did you get it?"

"Paulo lent it to me."

"Why do you need a car?"

"It's a loan to do some errands for Paulo."

"I don't like your friendship with him. He isn't a good influence for a kid."

"Ma, I'm not a kid, I'm almost eighteen."

"Yes, I know. I was there when you were born."

"Yeah, very funny."

"I never knew much about your father's dealings with Paulo, but I suspected they were into something wicked." Her voice softened. "Please be careful. That's all I'm asking."

"When I save enough money we'll rent a small house. Just for the three of us." He embraced her.

* * *

As usual, Gloria sewed with the radio on. She loved to listen to tangos played by an accordion because her husband had enjoyed performing for her on that instrument. They spent lovely evenings together; he played his favorite tangos, and she sang for him. Almost two years after his passing, the memory of her husband still hurt. She didn't sing tangos, anymore.

Life must go on. It always does. No matter if you are hurting, she told herself.

Gloria came back from her daydream as Antonio stood by the door holding a medium size box.

"Hi, Ma."

"What's that?" she said, looking at the box.

"Something for you. Open it."

She did. It was a small television set.

She gasped. Her deep-set eyes quizzed him. "Where did you get this?"

"At a store. I bought it for you."

"Where did you get the money?"

"I got paid from the hardware place."

"I know they don't pay well there. Tell me the truth."

"I've been working there for over a year. My employer gave me a bonus because I do a good job. I keep the books, I look after customers, and I even mop the floors. Why do you always doubt me, Ma? That's hurtful."

A meek smile appeared on her face. "Sorry, *amor*, I didn't

mean to hurt you. But I'm concerned about you making the right choices."

"Don't worry, I won't disappoint you."

* * *

Paulo drove his BMW through the unpaved streets of the poor Argentine barrio.

It was almost obscene to drive such a fancy car in that impoverished neighborhood. Once he arrived at Gloria's communal home, he parked his vehicle on the side of the road. A scrawny child wearing ragged pants and a frayed top stared at the car in awe.

"Hey, kid, if you keep an eye on my car, I'll give you five *pesos*," Paulo shouted.

"Si, patron," the child replied, jumping up and down.

Paulo grabbed a bag of groceries and a bunch of flowers from the back seat of his car and went to the house to knock on Gloria's door. When she opened it and saw his smiling face, nausea swirled in her stomach.

There he is again, pretending to be nice but hiding his true intentions, she thought.

"Hello, there," he said, grinning.

"What are you doing here?"

"May I come in?"

She said nothing.

He walked in and put down the bag of groceries on the only table in the room.

"What's that?" she asked, pointing to the bag.

"I walked by the supermarket and got a few groceries, you know, for you and the boys," he said with a smirk.

"I don't want them. I don't need your charity. Please, take them away," she said, raising her chin in defiance.

"Come on, Gloria, don't be like that." He came closer.

"And take those flowers to your wife. I don't want them either."

A nasty glint turned his eyes to stone. "So, you think I'm not good enough for you, is that it? I got Antonio a job at the store, and I'll help Bruno too. You owe me. You better be nice to me."

She backed away from him but he pushed her against the wall, kissed her neck, and tried to get his hand between her legs.

Gloria felt his heavy breath on her face. Her heart raced with panic.

At that moment, Antonio entered the room. He couldn't believe his eyes: Paulo, trying to take advantage of his mother? Blackness blinded his reasoning. His eyes bulged with rage and he threw himself against the older man. Paulo reacted quickly; he curled his hand into a fist and aimed for Antonio's face. His fist hit the bridge of the young man's nose. Antonio's blood splattered all over the floor.

"Stop, please, stop! Gloria shouted." She stood between Paulo and her son. "Leave him alone," she pleaded. She helped Antonio to stand. He wiped his bleeding nose with his shirt sleeve.

Paulo warned him, "Stupid kid. If you ever touch me again, you'll pay with your life."

Trembling, Gloria shouted, "Get out of here, *mierda*!"

Huffing, Paulo stomped out of the room, dashed to his car and drove away.

Gloria took Antonio to the local hospital to receive care. He was sent home the same day to recover.

* * *

While resting, Antonio found himself worrying about his younger brother. Bruno was gullible and impulsive. Antonio didn't like the friends his brother hung around with.

Those boys were much older than Bruno. They smoked cigarettes or pot when they could get their hands on some. They also drank in front of anyone who cared to watch. The group gathered at an empty lot a few blocks from where Bruno's family lived.

Antonio's musing was interrupted as he glanced at his brother getting ready to leave.

"Hey, where are you going?"

"I'm gonna meet my friends. Why?" Bruno shot him a steady look.

"You did your homework? You should finish your schoolwork before going out."

"You are not my father to tell me what to do."

"I know. But since Pa is dead, you are my responsibility now."

"I don't care. You are not my boss." He shrugged and curled his upper lip in disdain.

"Listen, I don't want you to hang around with those losers. I want to keep you safe."

"I don't need you to babysit me. I'll be sixteen soon," Bruno said and stomped out of the room.

Antonio punched his fist into his palm in frustration. He needed to protect his brother.

* * *

After witnessing Paulo's behavior toward his mother, Antonio decided to quit working for him. He needed to get away from the old man and his dealings.

When they met again, Antonio had to contain his disgust at seeing Paulo. It was the first time they'd spoken after their fight.

Before leaving Paulo's place, Antonio asked him, "Could I have a word with you?"

"What do you want?" His voice sounded harsh.

"I'm letting you know this is my last delivery. I'm quitting."

"Good. I was about to tell you the same. I don't want to work with useless guys like you."

"I don't care what you think. I'm glad we're done." He turned and left, relieved his business with Paulo was almost finished.

I should never have gotten involved in this. What

would've happened to Ma and Bruno if I got hurt or killed? Never mind, that'll be all in the past soon, he thought.

* * *

For some time, Ramirez kept working on the strategy to dismantle Paulo's operation. He'd involved a police officer who physically resembled Chino. The officer wanted to be present when the raid occurred, not only to see that the operation ran smoothly but also to savour his accomplishment of putting the criminals behind bars. Another delivery would give him a chance to nab the delinquents.

The day of the final delivery arrived, wrapping Antonios' heart in unrest and anticipation. His sweaty palms almost slipped from the steering wheel while driving. He made his way to the back alley to wait for the delivery. Anxiously, Antonio waited at the usual place. This last deal meant some extra money to save.

Minutes passed, but Chino didn't show up. Perspiration ran down Antonio's face. He cracked his knuckles, and his dry tongue stuck to his palate.

"This imbecile is always late," he murmured.

"It's about time," he shouted at Chino when he saw him approach.

Then, he realized, although the man looked like Chino, it wasn't him.

"Chino couldn't come. I'm doing his job today," the guy said.

Antonio's heart pounded. Sweat dampened his upper lip. Glancing at the stranger for a few seconds he had a hunch he was a cop.

Panic clouded his mind. He sprinted away and tossed his gun down an alley. The police officer got his weapon out, shouting, "Stop, or I'll shoot!"

Antonio ran a short distance until a sharp pain on the side of his lower left leg stopped him. He fell to the ground. The officer got to him and searched for a gun, but he had none. By then, Ramirez had arrived. He inspected Antonio's leg and found it was a small graze with minimal bleeding.

"Stupid boy, you could've been killed. You're lucky the bullet missed your leg. You just got a scrape. We'll go to Paulo's place, anyway."

Ramirez cuffed Antonio and pushed him into the car's backseat. The other officer sat in the passenger side, and they departed.

* * *

Meanwhile, Paulo paced his garage holding his phone. He dried one clammy hand on the side of his jeans. He bit his lower lip until a couple of blood drops ran down his chin. *Son of a bitch,* he thought, *I'm gonna kill him! I'm glad I won't see his face after tonight. To hell with Gloria and her boys.*

His phone's screen lit up. "I'm here."

Paulo activated the remote control to open the garage

door. The two policemen appeared by the side of the entrance and took him by surprise.

"Halt! Hands over your head. Now!"

Paulo reached for his gun and shot Ramirez. The other officer returned fire. A bullet hit Paulo in the chest and he fell to the ground. As he lay sprawled on the floor, a small pool of blood formed by his side.

The policeman ran to Ramirez, who was bleeding profusely from his arm. The officer called for help.

"Don't you move a muscle," he said to Antonio, who remained frozen in the car, holding his leg. The young man didn't dare to utter a word.

After a short while, the ambulance arrived. The attendants pronounced Paulo dead at the scene. They transported Ramirez and Antonio to the hospital.

* * *

In the emergency room, a young doctor examined Antonio's leg while a policeman kept guard at his door. Gloria and Bruno stood by his side.

"You'll be fine. This is a superficial wound, but I'll give you a prescription for antibiotics to prevent infection. The nurse is going to dress it for you."

"Thanks, Doctor," he said.

The policeman approached his bed. "When the nurse finishes, I'll take you to the station to give your statement."

He nodded. "May I ask you something?"

"Go ahead."

"How is the other officer doing?"

"He is being looked after. The doctor said he'll recover."

"I'm glad," Antonio said.

Through an open window, Gloria heard an accordion playing a tango. Soft music permeated the room. She recognized the melody; it was one of her husband's favorites. She remembered the title, "Life Aways Begins Tomorrow."

BEHIND THE CURTAIN

As part of her daily routine, Chalai went to the temple to pray to Buddha. She had so much to ask him. She prayed for her mother's health, for her older sister Nui living in Australia, for her father's soul and, above all, she prayed for herself. She asked him to protect her from evil spirits and to guide her on the right path.

The incense sticks she held illuminated her beautiful features. A month ago she turned twenty. She had flawless skin, a tiny mouth, and enchanting slanted eyes. A cascade of straight black hair ran down her back.

Chalai knelt in front of the statue of a Walking Buddha. It was her favourite because this Buddha's right hand was raised in a gesture of reassurance. Also, the statue emphasized his earthly aspects. She put down a fruit offering at his shrine and left the temple.

She strode to her job on Khaosan Road where she worked at a small massage parlor located between an internet café and a bookshop. Coming from Ubon, her home city of about one hundred thousand, to Bangkok, a metropolis of over eight million, had been an overwhelming experience. She shared a room at Miss Anong's home, a humble boarding house on the outskirts of Bangkok.

Kannika, her roommate, an introverted girl about the same age as Chalai, also came from Ubon. In the beginning, Kannika wasn't prone to small talk, but as time went by, the two girls became friends. It intrigued Chalai how Kannika managed her earnings because her roommate never seemed to be short of money. But Chalai thought it wouldn't be polite to ask about it.

Chalai had been working at the parlor for about six months. Miss Dao, the owner, liked her. She talked to her in a gentle tone and gave her fair pay. But money was always short. After paying rent to Miss Anong, getting groceries, and sending money to her mother, there wasn't much left.

She missed her sister Nui. Barely a year older, they used to share most things, a bed, house chores, clothing, and dreams. Nui used to work as a waitress at a restaurant in downtown Bangkok. There, she met an Australian man, twenty-five years her senior.

After a short courtship, he asked her to move to Australia

with him. She liked him enough to accept his offer. But above all, she wanted to be looked after by a man with means, who could offer her a better life than the one she had in Thailand.

Nui got in touch with her family often at the beginning, but after a while her phone calls and letters became infrequent. However, she dutifully sent her mother money.

Chalai missed her sister and often wondered about her life in Australia. Was she happy?

But Chalai had her own dreams. She thought of her job at the parlor as temporary. She wanted more out of life. Her main dream was to emigrate to Australia, as her sister had done. She'd heard people talking about a wonderful country, stunning beaches, and a good economy. She dreamed about living there.

Someday, if her dream came true she'd bring her mother, so she could take care of her.

Maybe, just maybe, she would meet a good man and start a family of her own.

When Chalai got to her place, Miss Anong was waiting for her.

"It's good you're home, I'm concerned about Kannika."

"What happened?"

"I'm not sure, but she didn't want to eat and she's been crying."

"I'll go and see her."

Chalai knocked softly on the door. Kannika was lying on the bed, head under a pillow sobbing quietly. Chalai came closer, gently touching her friend's head. "What is the matter?" Silence. Kannika didn't move.

"You miss your family? Are you sick? May I help you in any way?" she asked.

"No, you can't help me. No one can."

"Why do you say that?"

"I'm pregnant." Kannika's voice sounded curt and abrupt.

"But you don't have a boyfriend. How can you be pregnant?"

As she dried her tears, Kannika folded her arms over her stomach. "Oh, Chalai, you are so naive."

Dragging nails down her cheeks, Kannika added, "I can't have this baby. It'd bring dishonor to my family"

"Can't the baby's father help you?"

"I don't know who the father is."

"What do you mean?"

"I'm a sex worker."

Chalai's eyes grew big. She opened her mouth in a silent exclamation.

"You want me to spell it for you?" Kannika asked.

Chalai returned her friend's frown with a little hostility. "I know what a sex worker does"

"No, you don't. Do you think I enjoy this? I hate it with all my heart."

"Why do you do it, then?

Kannika sighed, rolled her eyes, and said, "Because I need the money to send to my family. I have five younger siblings and my parents to look after. They are counting on me to get by."

Tilting her head, Chalai asked, "What are you going to do?"

* * *

It was night. The two girls walked down a dark alleyway on the periphery of Bangkok. When they reached the address they'd been given, they stopped and scanned their surroundings, the semi-darkness menacing. The location reeked of unattended garbage.

Trembling and holding hands they entered a small, dark waiting room of a back-street place. The paint on the walls was peeling off and the floor looked unkempt. A tattered piece of fabric hung from the ceiling like a curtain. No one was there.

"This place looks sinister," Chalai whispered.

"You can leave now if you want, you know"

"No, I wouldn't leave you here all by yourself."

"Thanks, Chalai."

"Good evening ladies. Who is having the job done?"

The voice belonged to a slight man, wearing a stained, off-white lab coat. He had a long gray beard and crooked teeth.

"That's me, Doctor," Kannika's voice quivered.

"I'm not a doctor, child, but I can help you."

Kannika didn't reply. She couldn't utter a word, her chin and lips trembling.

"Do you have the money?"

Her small hands shook uncontrollably when she gave him the bills. After counting the money, he touched her elbow. "Come with me. It won't take long."

Chalai noticed he had dirty nails.

Kannika and the little man left the room and disappeared behind the curtain.

Chalai paced the floors, biting her nails, praying while waiting for Kannika to reappear from behind the curtain. But when it opened, she didn't see her friend. Instead, the man, now wearing a bloody apron stood there, panic written all over his face.

He shouted, "Get your friend out of here! She needs a hospital! Too much bleeding!"

She ran to Kannika's side, helped her off the bed, and dragged her to the street screaming. "Help, help!"

No taxis were around. A *tuk-tuk* passed by, but it didn't stop.

The next morning, Chalai went to the temple to pray to Buddha. She had so much to ask him. She prayed for her mother's health, for her older sister Nui returning to Bangkok and for her father's soul.

But, most of all, she prayed for Kannika's spirit, looking after her from heaven.

TIME NEVER FORGETS

Angie knelt on the gardening pad and dug deep enough to prepare the ground to plant the rose bush. As she broke up the soil, her fingers touched something round and hard. She kept digging and brought it to the surface. It wasn't a pebble or a chunk of rock, as she initially thought. She dusted its surface, but not wearing her glasses, she didn't inspect the item any further and put it in her pants pocket.

A burning sensation on her back made her uncomfortable. It was seven a.m., but because of the unrelenting sun of the Australian mining town, it was already hot. By midday, the heat would probably hit its peak, reaching around forty degrees Celsius.

Angie, her husband Robert, and their son, Bob, had been living in the small mining town for over ten years. In the beginning, she wasn't sure if it was a smart idea to move to such a remote place, but for Robert, being in the police force was a good move. He'd earn better pay, housing was provided and their son would be raised in a country-style way of living, away from the dangers of big cities.

So far, it had worked well. Bob finished high school without major problems and was attending university in Perth. Angie worked as a librarian at the local school, and Robert ran the small police station.

Life was good.

She went back to the kitchen, had a glass of water, and rinsed the object in the sink. She reached for her reading glasses and inspected the item carefully.

It was a locket.

She opened it and discovered a picture of two mature people. The man's scanty whitish hair, the woman's timid smile, and the picture's faded sepia intrigued her. She analyzed their features. Despite being an old photograph, she could clearly see their Asian heritage.

She waited until Robert came back from work.

"Hi, honey," Robert said, throwing his police hat on the hall table.

"Hello, darling," she said and kissed him. Despite all the years they'd been together, it felt so good to kiss his lips. "You had a good day?"

"Yeah, the usual. Parents complain about their kids' bikes being taken from their front yard, and a dumb fight between neighbors because dogs cross their property. That kind of thing. What about you?"

"Fine. I planted new rose bushes this morning."

"Oh, good."

"Look what I found buried in the backyard," she said as she reached into her pocket.

He took the locket from Angie's hands. He observed the object carefully, brought a shaky hand to his forehead, and leaned against the wall.

"What's wrong, honey?" she asked.

"Nothing," he said when he could breathe.

"What do you mean, nothing? You almost passed out. Have you seen this locket before?"

He couldn't articulate a sentence.

"Please, Robert, you're scaring me."

"I buried the locket a few years ago."

"Why did you do that?"

"I did it for Bob."

"What?"

"It's a long story, Angie."

"I'm listening."

He walked to the sofa and sat, head down, hands on his knees. The hum of the air conditioning filled the room. Angie stood in front of him, arms crossed over her chest, tapping her right foot impatiently.

"Please, take a seat. You're making me nervous."

"Am I?" She could feel her brow furrow.

"I'll tell you everything from the beginning, but I want you to listen carefully, because this is about Bob."

She sat in front of her husband, watching his face.

"You remember the party his friends threw for him when he turned eighteen?" he said.

"Yeah. I wasn't here because we had a shopping trip to the city with a couple of girls from work."

"That's right."

He stood and paced the floor. "As a birthday present, Bob's friends hired an exotic dancer from Perth."

"What? Did you know about it beforehand?" She raised her voice.

"No, I didn't. Calm down and listen, honey. The dancer was a young girl from Thailand. She had been in the country for a short while and was saving money to bring her parents here someday."

"I don't see how this girl's story is related to the locket." Losing patience, Angie squirmed in her seat.

He continued."I left the boys on their own and went for a beer. The girl hadn't arrived yet."

"So, you never saw her?"

"I did."

"When?"

"Later. I was finishing my second beer when Bob came into the pub huffing. He was out of control."

"What happened?"

He came close to her and touched her shoulder. "He told me the girl was dead."

Angie covered her mouth with both hands to stifle a gasp.

Robert walked to the window and gazed at the backyard. The red bougainvillea they planted ten years ago stood as a silent witness to his despair. He closed his eyes and rubbed his temples.

"Tell me, what happened." Her voice trembled.

"Bob and the boys did some drugs. So did the girl. Maybe it was her first time and she overdosed. I don't know. They tried to revive her, but they couldn't. She was about Bob's age."

Angie couldn't stop a guttural sound from escaping her mouth. "Oh, poor child." She left the room sobbing.

Robert collapsed on the sofa. *I have to tell her the whole truth. There is no going back now.*

Taking a short walk in the garden, Angie composed herself and found her way back to the living room. She sat beside Robert and looked straight ahead to avoid his eyes.

"What happened next?"

"When we came back from the pub, the girl's body was lying on the floor in Bob's room."

"What did you do with her?"

His chin quivered. "We did what we had to. We buried her."

"Oh, God. I can't believe what I'm hearing. Who are you? You got rid of her like a piece of trash? You're a police officer, for Christ's sake!"

"It was the only option to save Bob."

"Why?"

"I couldn't take her to the hospital for an autopsy. He had sex with the girl. The coroner could've traced her death to Bob. You understand now?"

"No, and I never will."

She scurried to the spare room. Her head spun, a dull pain settled in her heart, and she fell on the bed. "Oh my God, this is so terrible! What am I going to do?"

She got an old album from the bookcase. After turning a few pages, she found the pictures she was looking for: Bob's third birthday, his first day at school, him standing beside his three-wheeler bike. All the images showed a little boy smiling at his mother's face. So many pictures, and so many memories.

* * *

The next morning, as Angie opened her eyes, bright rays of sunlight filtered through the curtain. It was the first time she'd slept in the spare bedroom. She missed having Robert's warmth by her side.

The smell of fresh coffee permeated the kitchen.

"Morning, honey. I have breakfast ready."

"Thanks, I'm not hungry. I'll just have coffee."

He poured a cup and gave it to her. "Tell me about the locket," she said.

"I found it under the rug in the living room the next day.

I didn't know what to do with it. I wasn't thinking straight and I buried it in our backyard. That was stupid."

"So, you planned not to tell me about this, ever?"

"What was the point, love? I didn't want you to go through hell as I did."

He took her hands in his. "I'm so sorry, honey. I love you."

"Where is she buried?"

"In the old mine site. No one goes there."

Angie took the locket and opened it. It seemed like the old couple was looking straight into her eyes. "They must've been her parents," she said with empathy.

He nodded in agreement.

"Take me to her burial site. They would like to be close to their daughter," she said.

* * *

Early the next morning, the sun was already out, warm and pleasant. They knew its sensation would be short-lived.

They drove to the old mining site in silence, both deep in thought. *What would parents do to protect their children?* Angie wondered. She gazed at Rob. He didn't meet her eyes.

"We're almost there," he said, his demeanor somber.

After a couple of minutes, Rob stopped the jeep and got out. Angie followed him until he stood in front of the group of stones beside a jacaranda. The tree with its blue trumpet-shaped flowers, fern-like leaves, and fragrant timber was common in the Australian bush.

Angie reached for her pocket and took out the locket. She knelt under the tree and dug with both hands into the reddish dirt, still soft after the rain the day before. Rob knelt beside her to help.

After they dug the small hole, Angie placed the locket within and covered it up.

"We should offer a prayer," she said.

They did.

As they went back to the car, Angie gazed at the jacaranda tree once more, but tears got in the way.

LUCIA

"Manolo, I need you to collect logs at night because wood that is cut by the full moon burns better," Mother said while stirring a large iron pot, hanging from the ceiling of the hut.

"*Si*, Mama. I'll help you when I'm back from town." Even at eighteen, people said my head full of curls encircled a childish-looking face.

"What are you going to do there?"

"I want to see the traveling band; I like their music and dancing."

"You go to see the girls, right?" She raised an eyebrow. Mama was a small-framed woman who wore her scarce white hair in a thin braid. Her calloused hands spoke of hard work. Her face revealed a trail of sadness but her eyes sparkled every time she looked at me.

"Not all girls, Mama, just one."

She and I lived a precarious existence, owing only a few possessions to make life tolerable. She took care of the little orchard and I herded sheep. The simplicity of our ordinary days lasted until the flamenco traveling band got into town. Musicians and dancers arrived carrying around their belongings: their tents, their children, their guitars and drums.

* * *

Late that night, under a starry sky and a full moon as a silent spectator, I heard the music once again. The electrifying flamenco rhythms resonated in my head and heart. An invisible rope pulled me towards the music. The intoxicated rhythm played by those captivating instruments touched every fiber of my soul, enhancing my senses.

Following the sound, I got close to the tent. I saw them sitting next to a bonfire. A young man played his guitar with such passion I thought he would've been happy to keep playing with bleeding fingers.

I had seen Lucia dance a few months ago, when the band came to our village and I sneaked through their tent to watch. Countless bracelets adorned her wrist which seemed to sing a captivating melody as she moved her hands. I was close enough to observe her eyes. There was something deeply hidden in her gaze. Maybe a hint of malice or a demonic power in those pitch-black eyes. She stared at me.

Since then, she had been a constant presence in my dreams. I was infatuated with her and there was nothing I could do about it. Maybe she bewitched me.

And there I was again, waiting to see her dance once more. From my hidden place, blood rushed through my veins. I took a deep breath to steel myself.

Then, as if emerging from the flames, Lucia walked to the center of the circle ready to dance. Eyes closed, she waited for the music to fill her soul. Absorbing the rhythm, she danced to the cadence of the crying guitar.

Her suggestive movements were full of sensuality, vibrancy, exuberance and tenderness. The music reached a crescendo while the insinuating movements of her upper body clouded my reasoning. Every time I gazed at the deepness of her eyes, a wave of desire swept through me.

What a delirious seduction of the senses!

Lucia's body followed the exhilarating music, and in a histrionic ending, she dropped to the ground at my feet. I thought my heart would explode. I fell under a spell. With a swift movement, I tried to help her get up. As I did, Lucia grinned and touched my cheek. The blood throbbed under my skin. Without thinking, I grabbed her by the waist and stole an urgent passionate kiss from her full red lips. I let her go in an instant, feeling embarrassed. Her eyes flickered like the sky before the storm.

She laughed at me and said in a raspy, seductive voice, "Come to my tent tonight."

Cheeks burning and heart thumping, I couldn't talk. My heightened senses didn't allow me to think of anything else but her command.

* * *

Darkness blanketed the small village. The wind blew widely, breaking branches and scaring dogs. Rain fell strong and steady. As I made my way to Lucia's tent, I was almost inebriated by love, lust and anticipation. I stood at the tent's entrance, my legs turned to jelly. I took a deep breath and walked in.

She waited for me. Without saying a word, Lucia approached me and tenderly placed her hand on the nape of my neck. I perceived the faintest of blushes creeping up my face. Her scent invaded my senses, muddling my reasoning and enhancing my desire. She kissed me passionately.

When I caught my breath, I said, faintly, "I'm ready for love."

Lucia's voice was intoxicating. "I'll be yours if you grant me a wish."

Enraptured by her, I said, "I will do whatever you ask."

"I want you to bring me your mother's heart."

For a few moments, my lungs refused to work. What was she asking? She looked at me with those penetrating and malevolent pitch-black eyes. Against all reasoning, I knew then that her wish must be granted.

* * *

I ran through meadows and hills until I arrived at my place. My mind was empty, only Lucia's voice kept repeating her macabre wish. My movements were mechanical. I grabbed the axe next to the pile of small logs outside our hut.

My mother, hunched over the kitchen table, didn't hear me coming. A single blow was all it took to get my mother's body at my feet in a pool of blood. In my head, it was as if time had stopped.

I raced back to Lucia's tent with my deadly offering.

In my frenzy, I tripped on a rock. Then, my mother's heart asked, "Oh, my son, are you hurt?"

"Sorry, Mother," I replied.

WHAT THE MIRROR TELLS

Alice turned seventy-five a few months ago. Life was so empty. They were times when she just wanted to be done with it.

It wasn't the first time she intended to finish with everything. When Alfred passed away, after fifty years of marriage, she didn't want to keep going.

Waking up and touching the empty space on their bed caused her intolerable pain. His scent permeated the whole bedroom, his closet and their bathroom. She didn't even know for how long she'd cried, hugging his pillow.

Her loneliness was in part made bearable because of Cecilia's visits. Her grandmother had passed away a long time ago, but she appeared to her in dreams, giving her comfort and solace. The same way she did when Alice was a little girl and scraped her knee.

On one of those nights, when sleep escaped Alice, her

grandmother's voice whispered to her, "Darling, I know you're hurting, but trust me, you'll learn to live with the pain of losing Alfred. It will take time for your wound to heal."

Somehow Alice kept going. She had to, for Andrea, her only child. It sounded funny to think of Andrea as a child. She was a thirty-seven-year-old married woman. Alice loved her, as mothers do–unconditionally. It's a blind love because whatever you go through, you keep loving. She did love her husband very much, but her love was conditional. The condition was based on mutual respect, which meant being faithful. She kept that promise, and she wanted to believe Alfred had too.

She shook her head, as if that gesture could put away her thoughts. She made her way to the porch to water her potted plants when Andrea's car pulled up the driveway.

"Hi, Mom. How're you doing?" She kissed Alice's cheek.

"Hi, baby, I'm good. It's great to see you."She hugged her. "How are you feeling? Your tummy is getting bigger."

"I know," Andrea said, caressing her abdomen. "I'm fine, but so thirsty, Mom." She licked her lips.

"Let's go inside. I made fresh lemonade."

They entered the kitchen where Andrea sat, elbows on the kitchen table, and looked around. "Mom, this place needs some work. You have to replace the appliances, and you should paint the ceiling."

Alice smiled, offering her daughter a glass of lemonade. She grabbed a chair and sat by her daughter's side. "I know this kitchen would look better with new appliances, but I don't need them, love. Everything works fine"

"Mom, since Dad passed, this place has been falling apart, but if you don't want to keep it up, that's fine. It's your house."

"I'm happy here. Don't worry about me. How are things going with you?"

"Good. The babies are growing well. I still can't believe I'm having twins. Soon I won't be able to drive anymore."

"That's not a problem. I'll take you places."

"Thanks, Mom." Andrea inspected her hands carefully. "I don't know how I am going to cope looking after twins. People say it's hard having one baby, never mind two."

"I'll help, you know."

"Yeah, I know. But I'll need you all the time." She looked at her mother, pleading.

In her daughter's tone, Alice sensed a hidden meaning. She took Andrea's hands in hers. "Everything is going to be fine."

"Mom, when the babies are born I'd like you to move in with us, for good. You should sell this house," she said in one breath.

"What?" Alice's eyes widened.

"Think about it. You could help me, you'll have your money. We'll be a large family. You know Christian likes you, and he's a good husband."

"Love, I don't want to move. My memories, my things are here. I'll go to your place every day to help with the twins.

We're not too far away. I'll stay with you for a while after they are born, but I don't want to sell my house. Sorry."

Andrea's face dropped. "I thought I could count on you."

"Of course, you can, but don't ask me to leave my home."

Andrea made her way out. "That's fine, if that's the way you feel!" she said and slammed the door.

* * *

After going over her situation for weeks, Alice felt compelled to do what she thought was her duty–to stand by her daughter. It was a painful process to get rid of the things she loved, but in the end, they were only that: things. She would carry her memories in her soul.

With a heavy heart, she moved into her daughter's home. *Life is all about adjusting to change, isn't it? I believe that's how the saying goes,* she thought.

Andrea waited for her mother at the main door. When Alice got out of the car, her daughter waddled to her side. "Hi, Mom. Thanks for this." She kissed her cheek.

"You're getting big and beautiful," Alice said.

"I don't feel beautiful, just very heavy. Come with me, Mom. I'll show you your room."

Alice's bedroom was ample, with plenty of light filtering through large windows. *"I'll be just fine here,"* she thought.

* * *

Time passed quickly, and Andrea had a normal delivery. The baby boys were a bit early, so they had to stay in the nursery for observation, but they were released after a few days.

It was challenging for Andrea to look after her twins, especially in the first weeks, but having Alice by her side made everything easier.

After her maternity leave was over, Andrea had to return to work. Alice looked after her grandchildren; it was exhausting but she was content to help the family by providing child-care.

One night, after putting the boys to bed, Alice noted her grandmother's silhouette against the dimming light of her bedside lamp. Cecilia's voice sounded clear and precise, "Love, I worry about you. Remember to take care of yourself, not just the children. If you don't look after your well-being, nobody will."

* * *

The boys grew happy and healthy under their grandmother's supervision.

When the boys turned three, things started to change.

As Alice was folding the boys' laundry, Andrea approached. "Mom, we have to talk." Her daughter's serious aspect concerned her.

"What is it about, love?"

"It's about your room. You'll have to move to the smaller

bedroom by the kitchen. Sorry, Mom. The boys need more space. Too many toys, I guess."

The request took Alice by surprise. "But that room is not big enough to hold my things."

"You'll have to make do, Mom. I wish we had a larger house, but we don't."

That was the end of the conversation. The next day, Christian and Andrea helped her to move her furniture to her new bedroom. The things that didn't fit were given to charity.

* * *

The following year, Alice's living arrangements had to change again. The boys kept fighting for space, so she had to give away her bedroom. This time there was no other room available but a narrow den beside the laundry room. The space was tiny, there was no window, no closet, just enough room for a single bed, a bedside table, and a small dresser. Alice had no choice but to move.

The older she got, the more she realized she wasn't included in the family affairs. Christian or Andrea weren't cruel to her. They were polite, but distant. The boys minded their own business and ignored her. At the table, the family talked over her without asking for her input. She felt lonely and displaced.

No one noticed she didn't eat properly. Because of her weight loss, her clothing hung loose, as if it didn't belong to her. Some days, showering was a big task, so she didn't. At times she preferred to stay in bed most of the day. But nobody in the family seemed to be aware of these changes.

If no one notices me, maybe I'm turning invisible, she thought.

* * *

The first time the revelation happened, it took her completely by surprise. She was reading a book on the porch. When she got up to make herself a cup of tea, she glanced at the large mirror in the hallway. There was no reflection.

She froze, feeling rooted to the spot, and looked into the mirror once more. A gasp caught in her throat. Panic flared in her chest. She squeezed her eyes shut. When she opened them her image was nowhere to be seen.

A loud scream escaped her mouth, filling the surroundings. She rushed to her room and closed the door. Sat on the side of her bed, grabbed the mirror on her nightstand table and searched for her reflection.

Instead of her features in the mirror, she saw the foggy image of her grandmother. Alice heard Cecilia's voice clearly, "My darling, I know you think you're becoming invisible, and maybe you are. Perhaps it's time to go. I'll be waiting for you on the other side whenever you're ready."

Alice smiled at the empty mirror and set it on her bedside table. She reclined on her bed and crossed her hands over her chest, expecting Cecilia's call.

A FAMILY AFFAIR

"I got a plan," Ethan said to Josh. "We should bury the box."

The sunless sky covered the forest over the treetops which created a canopy over their heads. Wind bustled through the branches of the trees. Chest heaving, the two boys dug with both hands the wet soil. Drops of perspiration bathed their young faces.

"What'll happen if Grandpa finds out what we've done? He'll beat the crap out of us. He doesn't love us and you know why." Josh bit his lower lip.

Ethan ignored his brother and kept digging.

When they finished, they put the box in the hole and covered the site with branches and debris they found around the area. They marked the site with a rock. Ethan held his younger brother's face with both hands, "You have to swear not to tell anyone about what we did."

Josh's eyes widened, "I swear," he said in a quivering voice.

Ethan, a thirteen-year-old and his brother Josh, who was eleven, lived with their

grandfather, Stanley, a widower, on a remote Ontario farm. They lost their mother when they were younger. After their father died in a car accident recently, the boys didn't have a choice but to go to live in the countryside which they disliked. The boys missed their parents, their friends and their school.

As they walked back to the house, in a nearby pond a frog croaked, like saying "I know your secret."

* * *

The two-story home was made of logs; its discoloured window frames and a peeling painted fence gave it a shabby appearance. Red pine trees surrounded the house; an old shed stood at the back of the property.

As they approached the house, two German Shepherds sprinted toward them. The dogs wagged their tails, barking and jumping up and down in welcome. The boys tried to restrain them, intending to sneak through the door and take the stairs once the dogs quieted down.

A loud voice startled them."Stop right there!" Their grandfather stared at them. His cold, flinty eyes scrutinized them. His face was barely visible wrapped in the cloud of smoke coming from his pipe. He stood from his creaky rocking chair and shuffling his feet he approached the boys.

"What were you up to?"

"Nothing, Grandpa," Ethan answered. Josh hid behind his brother.

"I bet you were up to no good," the old man sneered.

The boys looked at the floor.

"Go upstairs," Stanley said.

Before the accident, Ethan and Josh enjoyed spending time with their Grandfather. Stanley showed them how to milk a cow, how to clean the pigpen, how to herd the animals and other chores around the farm. It was fun to be around the old man. But all of that was in the past. The accident changed Stanley's heart; there was no doubt about it.

* * *

Stanley took another drag from his pipe. His forehead was deeply lined. Bushy gray eyebrows encircled his watery eyes. He walked to the mantel, gazed at James' picture, his only son, and immersed himself in thoughts.

He remembered the night of the accident vividly. It felt like it happened yesterday but it has been six months already. It had snowed the whole day and in some places, the tracks were coated in deep, partially frozen slush. They were in the car; he sat beside James, who was driving while the boys in the back seat kept fighting over a game. James turned his head for a second to tell them off when the car slid into a snowbank and it rolled upside down. Stanley woke up in a hospital bed, with a broken arm. The kids had cuts and bruises. A couple of days later, James died of internal bleeding. Stanley's heart broke into a million pieces. He tried to make sense of the situation. The accident wasn't the kids' fault. Or was it?

A solitary tear found its way to his lips.

* * *

Upstairs in their bedroom, the boys talked about what happened earlier.

"Grandpa will find out what we did. I'm scared," Josh said.

"Don't be. I'll protect you."

"He hates us," Josh insisted, his voice trembling. "You know he does."

Ethan ruffled his brother's hair, "we'll be ok," he said without conviction.

Deep in his soul, Ethan agreed with his brother. Their Grandpa didn't care for them. But, why? Many nights, awake in his bed, Ethan tried to find an answer. He wondered if their grandfather blamed them for the accident. Was that possible? No, of course not. That would be too horrible, the boy thought. Being older he felt responsible for his brother's well-being. He'll look after Josh, no matter what.

Ethan needed to figure out what to do about the box they buried in the forest.

. . .

The following day, a Saturday, the boys woke up early, had their breakfast and headed to the fields. There was always work to do around the farm. Picking up eggs from the coop, cleaning the pigsty and feeding the few cows their grandfather owned. When they finished, they washed up and ran to the house.

"I'm hungry," said Josh.

"I'll fix you something." Ethan followed his brother to the kitchen.

Sipping his coffee, their grandfather looked at them, "Are your chores done?"

"We finished, Grandpa."

"Good. I'm going to work in the shed. You better stay out of trouble." He grabbed his pipe and left.

After they finished eating the boys went to their room. Ethan sat by the side of his bed and took out a small photo album hidden under his mattress. Josh joined him. From the pictures, their father smiled at them.

* * *

Stanley spent most of the day in the shed, fixing tools and doing menial tasks. When he finished, he sat on a haystack to ruminate.

"I should get rid of that gun. It's dangerous to have it around, because of the boys. I'm going to bring it to town to hand it to the police."

He searched around for the wooden box, inside an old

cabinet, up on a shelf. Nothing. Forehead furrowed, he kept looking to no avail. His nostril flared and he pounded one fist into his palm. Grinding his teeth he left the shed.

He stomped into the kitchen looking for the boys. They weren't there. "Ethan, Josh, where are you?" He shouted.

Up in their bedroom, the boys heard him and hurried down. "You called us, Grandpa?" Ethan caught his breath. Josh stood beside his brother.

"You have something that belongs to me." The old man said sternly. "I want it back. Now."

"We don't know what you are talking about, Grandpa," Ethan said, red in the face.

The old man grabbed the boy roughly by the elbow. "Don't lie to me." His eyes scanned Ethan's face. "Where is the wooden box that was in the shed?"

Ethan didn't answer. His body stiffened.

"We buried it in the forest, Grandpa," said Josh. He started to whimper.

The old man gasped."Why on earth did you do that?"

"We wanted to get rid of the gun." Ethan's voice trembled. "We were afraid you

may hurt yourself."

"What...what?" The old man stuttered. "What are you saying?"

"We've seen in the movies that sometimes people do awful things to themselves when they're in pain." Ethan's eyes welled. "We know you miss Dad. We do too."

For a moment, Stanley's mind couldn't focus on what was

happening. He stared at the boy in amazement. Bewildered by the answer, he slumped onto a chair. Tipping his head back for a moment he fought back tears.

Then, the old man gazed at the boys. He realized he had been so immersed in James' absence that he couldn't see what was in front of his eyes. His grandchildren needed him and he was all they have. He understood he had been blind to the boy's pain and to their concern for him.

He came close to his grandchildren and wanted to say something wise that could explain his feelings, but he couldn't find the right words. Trying to compose himself, he said to the children with an emotion-rich voice, "We'll keep the box buried. It's going to be a family secret."

Ethan ran to his room and came back holding something behind his back. He said, "Grandpa, do you want to check out Dad's photo album?"

Stanley nodded.

The sun had already set and the first stars started to appear in the sky when the three of them sat around the fire to leaf through James' photo album.

Everything was right with the world in the end.

A White Lab Coat

Sara woke in his arms. She looked at him with adoring eyes as he slept soundly like a child after a day of playing.

She gazed at the package on top of the table and a shiver ran down her spine–it was her turn to do the delivery. She had done it before; it didn't matter. But the same feeling of apprehension filled her heart every time her turn came.

She slipped out of bed and showered. The aroma of fresh coffee and toast permeated the small apartment.

"Morning, darling. Got breakfast ready," Oscar said.

In answer, she kissed the tip of his nose.

"I don't have classes today," he said. "Maybe I could go with you to do the delivery."

"No, honey. I'll get more nervous if you're around. And you know it is not safe to have more than one person involved."

"You're right," he said and hugged her tightly.

She grabbed her backpack and the package.

"Don't forget the lab coat." He handed it to her.

"Thanks, babe," she said and left the apartment.

* * *

She strode a few blocks to catch the train. As usual, the subway station was crowded. Some day,

when she and Oscar finished their law degrees, they could move to a smaller location away from the big city. A quiet and peaceful place to raise the child they were expecting. But for now, that was a distant dream. More urgent matters occupied her mind.

She caught the train, got a seat, and covered the package with her coat. She closed her eyes and went over the instructions she had memorized.

"Get off at San Martin station," the man had said. "You should be there at ten a.m. sharp. Walk to the end of the platform, sit, and wait—your lab coat should be over your right arm. Shortly, someone should sit by your side. Don't look at the person. He or she must say, without looking at you, '1269, I like that number.' You'll have to say, 'I prefer 6912.' Stand up, leave the package on the seat, and walk away. Don't look back, walk briskly toward the exit, but don't run. In case you've been followed, take a few different buses before you go to classes."

She knew the instructions by heart. It wasn't her first

delivery, but this time was different. Why? A voice in her head answered the question.

Now it's not only my life in jeopardy, but also my child's life.

The operation went as planned. She never looked at the person, but she recognized a mature woman's voice. It wasn't only students facing danger; older people too.

After taking a couple of buses Sara was certain nobody had followed her. She went back to her college and attended regular classes. On her break she overheard a couple of girls talking.

"You know what happened to Luis?"

"No. I haven't seen him in a few days. It's not like him to miss classes."

"Her sister called me yesterday. She told me when Luis was walking home, he was taken and thrown into a car. A neighbor saw the whole thing and told his family."

"I feel for his mother. She probably won't see him again."

* * *

When Sara got home, she told Oscar about the conversation.

"I know Luis," he said. "He's a good student, but he takes too many risks."

Her voice trembled. "I'm afraid," she said, and they embraced.

"I've been thinking about what we talked the other day, you know," he said.

"Yeah, me too. It's going to be so hard to leave our families and friends. Everything we know and love is here." She dabbed a tear.

"I agree, *amor*. But we don't want our child to grow up in this horror."

"I know, you're right. Have you started the paperwork?"

"I already finished."

"Good."

"I'll get the coffee ready. The guys will be here any minute."

After a short while, someone knocked twice on the door. After five seconds there was another double knock. Sara opened the door, and a young man entered. She looked right and left to make sure nobody was around, then closed the door. She kissed her friend on the cheek. "Are you sure no one followed you?"

"I'm sure," he said. "Hello, Oscar." The two friends embraced.

Three other friends arrived at the apartment. Their meeting lasted a couple of hours. They talked about where to make the next deliveries, what to include in them and how to do them safely. At the end of the meeting, Oscar needed to say something. "Friends, Sara and I want to share with you our good news. We're expecting a baby."

"Congratulations," they said and hugged the couple.

"Thank you," said Oscar. "That's why Sara will do one more delivery, her last. After that, we will manage without her."

They all agreed with Oscar's decision. The friends left the apartment one by one, making sure nobody saw them and walked in different directions.

* * *

After a couple of weeks, it was Sara's turn to do her last delivery. The night before, after lovemaking she rested her head in the hollow of Oscar's arm.

"I'm scared," she said.

"Don't be, *amor*. Nothing bad is going to happen. I'll be close by this time."

"Good. I'll feel better having you around. I love you so much."

"Me too, darling. Go to sleep now."

She did. Having him by her side always made everything better.

Sara sat on the last bench at the subway station, her white lab coat on her right arm with the package under it. It was ten a.m. and nobody sat beside her. On the opposite platform, Oscar pretended to read a newspaper.

The train came and blocked his vision. When the train departed, she wasn't there. Oscar stood, running toward the exit and shouting for her. He saw her restrained by two men, and each of them grabbed her by an arm. He never stopped yelling her name.

When he got to the exit she was nowhere to be seen. He searched the other exits and the adjacent street calling her name like a madman.

* * *

If people live under a dictatorship there are no civil liberties. No democracy. No freedom of expression. No parliament. No free press. No judicial system. The concept is hard to grasp if someone hasn't lived in that situation.

Where could Oscar go to look for Sara? He checked every hospital, the local jails, and every morgue in the city. He found no answers. When he had nowhere else to go, he went to a church. It was the only place the military didn't overtly censor.

It didn't matter if someone practiced a specific faith. A person could be an atheist, an agnostic, or a devout Catholic, and the church would try to help. A group of social workers, lawyers, and volunteers worked under the church's supervision.

* * *

It took him over two years to find her. Thanks to an anonymous tip, the church discovered an unmarked grave with four bodies in it. Using DNA samples and dental records, they identified the corpses.

Sara's cranium had a hole in her right temple.

What was in those packages? Political propaganda against the oppressive regime. The students made the pamphlets using an old press Oscar hid in their apartment. They read: "We want free elections." "Stop the killings." "Freedom." "Where are our missing loved ones?"

The wind brought the messages to every corner of the city. The leaflets flew like white doves carrying a message of hope.

Datos de su cuenta de Internet

Habitación: 503

Propietario: NANCY MANCA

Cuenta: hbv25301@nauta.com.cu

Contraseña: 03508025

Tiempo: 90:00 Horas

A Ragdoll in a Garden

Teresa's stomach churned as she considered what she was about to do. It wasn't too late. She could still turn around and leave. She dried her sweaty palms on the side of her tight dress. Her borrowed pointy high heels squeezed her toes. The dress was cut too short for her liking but her friend had told her she should wear it. She glanced around the hotel, one of the most elegant in Mexico City.

"Nice place, right ?" A short man with a prominent belly and chubby hands approached her. The perspiration beading at the edge of his receding hairline shone under the corridor's dim lights. He smelled of liquor.

She took a deep breath. "Yes, it is." Her mouth was dry.

He called the elevator and pressed four. They walked down the hallway lined with lush carpet, moving toward room 403. Teresa's eyes darted right and left down the corridor, praying no one would see her.

"Something wrong?" He frowned.

"No, nothing's wrong."

A knot in her throat made it hard to breathe. Her knees shook and her heart raced like a runaway horse. She was afraid she might faint.

The man put the keycard in the door's slot. Entering, Teresa experienced a wave of guilt. To someone from a poor neighborhood, the place looked majestic. A large sitting area boasted two chairs with red velvet upholstery, a mahogany center table, a hanging chandelier and flower arrangements. A huge king-size bed with a delicate silk cover occupied the center of the room.

What am I doing here?

The knot in her throat tightened and her eyes welled up. The man put his hand on her shoulder and she blinked rapidly, startled by his touch. A shiver went up and down her spine.

"Would you like me to order some champagne?"

"Sure, sure." She refused to meet his eyes.

As he called for room service, she went to the bathroom, wetting her face with trembling hands. She couldn't stop shaking. The image in the mirror reflected Teresa's agonizing gaze. A sharp pang of guilt hit her in the middle of the chest and took hold of her.

"*You should be ashamed of yourself*," the image said.

"Yes, yes, I know." Teresa's tears blurred her vision.

"Why are you doing it, then?"

"When are you coming out?" On the other side of the door, the man paced the floor, a predator waiting for his prey.

"Give me a minute." A sheen of sweat broke out all over her body. She looked back at the mirror and thought of the talk she had with a girl from her university class. Teresa had mentioned she had trouble paying off her tuition, and the girl wanted to help.

"You could do what I do. You don't have to do it often and it pays very well."

"What do you do?"

"Solo tienes que abrir las piernas," the girl said.

"Open your legs?" It sounded demeaning, vulgar and rude. No metaphors or euphemisms could make it any less so.

Teresa left the bathroom as if in a trance and approached the bed. Her heartbeat resonated in her ears and her chest tightened. She blew out short breaths to gain control.

She closed her eyes and abandoned her body. Her spirit began the trip she took every time life showed its ugly side: her special place. Her garden was a haven of peace, her refuge, a sanctuary she created in her imagination where beauty and color abounded.

Spring had arrived with its vibrant colors and aromas. Hues of pink, mauve and yellow covered the garden. Roses, dahlias and calla lilies reminded her of the small garden in the modest house that sheltered her childhood, in Chiapas, her distant home. Life was so easy then, all its mysteries yet to be discovered.

Meanwhile, her naked body remained sprawled on that hotel bed, like a ragdoll. When Teresa opened her eyes, the faint aroma of lavender suffused the air.

THE SECRET IS IN THE SAUCE

Chiara gathered what she needed to start cooking: onions, garlic, parsley, green peppers and spices. She peeled onions with no hurry, layer by layer. As the tears flowed down her face, she thought of *Nonna* Giulia. "When you're sad *bella,* it's a good idea to cook. You can cry all you want while you peel onions."

Cooking relaxed Chiara. The aroma of fresh herbs and ripe tomatoes from her grandmother's orchard brought memories of happier times.

Every Sunday her family had dinner at her mother's place. This time it was a special occasion-her mother's seventieth birthday.

I hope Gino is in a better mood tonight; lately, he's been acting so odd.

Chiara added fresh oregano and parsley to the sauce,

stirred it gently, closed her eyes and tasted it. The flavours dissolved in her mouth and she smiled.

This tastes heavenly. Nonna Giulia you are right; the secret is in the sauce.

As Chiara poured the sauce over the lasagna, she couldn't stop thinking about Sofia and the way she behaved. Chiara knew her sister was going to try to outdo her tonight, as she had for their entire lives. Always wanting the finest clothes, the ideal boyfriends, the best of everything.

It had been that way for as long as Chiara could remember; her sister always tried to outdo her. Sofia won, most of the time, but there was an area where Chiara shone–the kitchen. She was an outstanding cook. Sofia, a mediocre one.

But tonight's going to be different. My sauce will shine.

Chiara always felt close to *Nonna* Giulia when she cooked. Giulia had spent most of her time in the kitchen preparing mouth–watering dishes the whole family enjoyed: pasta con Pomodoro and Basilico, eggplant parm, sausage ragu, and Panzanella salad. Chiara and Sofia had absorbed every detail of the feasts their grandmother prepared on Sundays.

Gino's loud voice brought her back to reality.

"Don't tell me you're making pasta sauce again." He wrinkled his nose.

"I'm cooking for tonight's dinner at Mom's. She's turning seventy."

"I hate those dinners."

She bit her lip. "Please, hon, Mom's expecting us."

"Is Sofia going?"

"Yes, we'll all be there."

* * *

Sofia finished putting on her make-up and preened in her bedroom mirror. Her long, light-brown hair framed her beautiful face. She wore a fitted dress that accentuated her curvy figure.

"Well, I think I look splendid," she said, half-joking, half-serious.

A couple of years younger than Chiara, Sofia became aware of her stunning beauty at an early age. It served her well at school, and boys were crazy about her. Not only was she a good student, popular and liked by her teachers, but her parents had pampered and over-protected her.

But, *Nonna* Giulia cautioned her, "Careful *bambina,* beauty is not enough. You should have a kind heart."

At her mother's birthday, Sofia wanted to impress everyone with a sauce of her own creation. She got the recipe from an Italian chef, a friend of hers, but the family didn't need to know it. On such a special occasion, it'd be her chance to finally best her sister.

* * *

Francesco kissed Sofia's naked shoulder. "You look ravishing, darling," he whispered in her ear. He stared at her misty-eyed and tried to hug her.

"Cut it out," she protested."You're messing up my hair."

"Sorry, honey, I don't want to upset you."

"For God's sake, stop apologizing." She sighed loudly and turned away.

I hate when Francesco apologizes for everything he thinks he does wrong. I believe he feels jealous of every young man who looks at me. It's not my fault if he's twenty years older and boring.

When they got married, Sofia thought she was in love. But, soon she lost interest. Francesco's wealth helped at the beginning. She enjoyed spending money, but her life with him was devoid of enjoyment and passion.

* * *

Chiara stepped out of the shower. Her short auburn hair and attractive figure made her look younger than her age. She observed her reflection in the bathroom mirror. She touched her breasts and caressed her stomach.

I'm thirty-nine, and I'm not getting any younger.

"You startled me," she said as her hand flew to her chest.

"I bet you were daydreaming," Gino said while fidgeting with his tie.

"No, I was just thinking."

"About what?"

"About starting a family," she said, her voice trembling.

"How many times do we have to go over this?" He rubbed the back of his neck. "You knew I didn't want kids. I made it clear before we married."

"Yes, I know. But I do. Would it be so bad to start a family?"

"Just drop it. Don't want to talk about it."

Chiara rubbed her eyes, hiding her tears. "Fine. But we're not done with this."

Chiara and Gino arrived at Rosa's place. They walked through the garden. Chiara stood under the old lemon tree her father had planted long ago. She thought of her father and his kind smile. So many memories came to mind. She saw herself running around the patio, chasing her little poodle. Those were good days. Too bad they were gone forever.

"Ciao Mamma," Chiara said, entering the kitchen. She hugged her mother tenderly.

"Ciao, bella." Rosa kissed her daughter on the lips.

"The garden looks pretty. And your veggie patch too."

"Grazie mille, mia cara. Since your papa has gone, I have lots of time to garden. Anyway, I like fresh herbs for my cooking. What did you bring for tonight?"

"I made a lasagna, with a special sauce."

"What a coincidence. Sofia brought one too."

"Oh no, I should've asked first."

"It doesn't matter. No two lasagnas are the same. The secret is in the sauce, as your *nonna* used to say"

"Yeah, I remember." Chiara smiled and left to set the table.

Sofia and Francesco arrived shortly after. Sofia kissed her mother and stood in front of her, hands on her waist.

"How do I look, *Mamma*?" She twirled around.

"You look dazzling as always, *mia cara*."

"Thank you." She gave a childish giggle.

"I saw Gino's car," Sofia said.

"Yes, he and Chiara just got here."

"I'm gonna help her," Sofia hurried out of the kitchen.

"Hey, Chiara."

"Hey there." Chiara turned to face Sofia. "I like your outfit."

"Oh, this old thing," said Sofia, arranging her skirt. She grabbed glasses from the dining room cabinet. "Let me give you a hand."

"No need, I'm almost done."

"Okay, then, if you say so. *Mamma* told me you also brought lasagna."

"I did." Chiara bit her lip.

"Well, sorry to say this, but mine is going to shine. I've used a new sauce. Found a great recipe." She fluffed her skirt once more.

"This isn't a contest Sofia," Chiara cracked her knuckles.

"It isn't? I thought it was," she walked out of the dining room laughing.

At dinner, Gino stood up, holding his wine-glass. "I'd like to propose a toast to my favourite mother-in-law. *Buon compleanno,* Rosa."

"Buon compleanno, Rosa," they all said in unison.

When they finished eating, Sofia asked, "Okay, *Mamma,* tell us which lasagna you enjoyed the most."

"I liked both." Rosa smiled at her daughters.

"Oh, come on, there must be one you preferred," Sofia insisted.

"Well, I thought the one in the white Pyrex had a wonderful flavor."

"That's mine!" Sofia said, clapping her hands.

Nighttime arrived at Rosa's place. A gentle breeze played with Sofia's hair as Gino's caressed her neck. She closed her eyes and cocked her head, as he squeezed her shoulder.

"I've missed you, you know." He grabbed her by the waist.

"I've missed you too. But we must be careful,"

"Are you going to talk to Francesco," he asked.

"You know I will, but I need to find the right time. What about Chiara?" she said.

"I'll talk to her soon," he said, touching Sofia's face.

. . .

Shortly after, Chiara entered the kitchen. Through the window, she saw them talking. She wondered why they were standing so close, and why their body language spoke of such familiarity.

Sofia looks so beautiful in that dress, and she likes to flirt. But it's all innocent, Gino loves her like a sister, she thought.

As days passed, the wall of coldness grew larger between Steve and Chiara. He hardly even talked to her. A veil of sadness and emptiness surrounded Chiara's life. She tried to fill that void by doing what she enjoyed most: cooking.

Thinking that a new style would help her distract from the misery of life, Chiara sign up for cooking classes with Madame Dubois, an older chef and owner of a renowned French restaurant. She was a small-framed woman, maybe in her late seventies, with cunning eyes and a soft smile.

With time, Chiara and Madame Dubois became friends.

One afternoon over a cup of tea, Chiara asked her, "Madame Dubois, how was your life back in France?"

"Oh, *cherié* I don't remember much." She observed her wrinkly hands.

"I bet you do," Chiara smiled.

"Well, okay. My family lived in a small town, close to Bordeaux. I married young. We had a small restaurant, but we lost it because of my husband's gambling. He also drank too much. He wasn't a good person." She twisted her mouth in a sour expression.

"I'm sorry that happened to you." Chiara pulled Madame Dubois into a side hug.

"Don't be sad. That's all in the past." She put a hand on Chiara's shoulder. "Go home now. It's getting late."

A full moon reigned in the sky when Chiara got home. The night was warm and enticing. She took a shower, wore a seductive nightgown and went to lie down beside Steve who was already in bed. She moved closer and caressed his naked chest. He turned on the television.

"You don't want to do that, do you?" Her voice sounded low and sultry.

He moved away. "Yeah, I do."

"What's the matter?" She came even closer.

"I'm tired, that's all," he turned up the volume.

"We haven't made love in a long time. Is anything wrong? Talk to me, please."

Gino took her hand and gazed into her eyes. "Yeah, we need to talk."

Her face turned pale and her breathing became labored. *This can't be good.*

"Let's be honest, Chiara," he said."We're in a loveless marriage and it isn't fair for you or me."

She couldn't believe her ears. "But I love you, I do," she said and pressed her lips tight.

Silence.

"We could make things work, you know. Let's give our marriage a chance. What about if we go to counseling?" she pleaded.

"Stop it. It won't work. It's too late for that." He got up to light a cigarette."We can't keep going like this. I don't think I love you anymore."

Sharp pain in her chest made it hard to breathe. "What?" she asked in disbelief.

"You heard me."

A lump formed in her throat. She had to ask."Are you in love with someone else?"

"No." He stared down at his fisted hands, and Chiara knew he was lying.

The next morning, Madame Dubois commented on Chiara's puffy eyes and sad demeanour.

"How are you *Ma cherié*?" she asked.

"Not great, not great at all." A heavy sigh escaped Chiara's mouth.

"If you need to talk, I'm here. I'm a good listener."

"Oh, Madame Dubois, you don't want to know."

"But I do, *cherié*. Sometimes talking helps."

"Okay, I'll say it straight, my husband is having an affair."

Madame Dubois's eyes widened. "Are you sure?"

"Yes, I am. I've found restaurant bills in his pockets. He locks himself in the bathroom to answer calls. I know he's seeing someone," said Chiara with a fluttering feeling in her belly. "A woman always knows," she added.

"Yes, I agree, *cherié*. I've been there."

"You have?" Chiara asked in disbelief.

"A long time ago, back in France, my husband had a mistress. I confronted him, and he hit me. I promised myself he'd never hurt me again–or anyone else"

"What happened to your husband?" Chiara's big brown eyes bulged.

"He died. A terrible accident," she said with a half-hearted shrug.

"How did it happen?"

"No one knows for sure. I made his lunch, he got quite sick, and the next day he was dead." She gave Chiara an odd look and added, "Food is a giver, but sometimes is a taker."

Learning French cuisine at Madame Dubois restaurant became more than a pastime for Chiara. She enjoyed the flavours, the aromas and the ambiance.

"Are you enjoying the classes, *cherié*?" Madame Dubois asked.

"I love them," said Chiara.

"That's good. You're a gifted cook. Would you like to work for me?"

A silent oooh escaped Chiara's mouth. "That'd be a dream. But I already have a job."

"I know. But you could work for me for a couple of evenings and the occasional weekend."

"Well, it sounds like a plan." She embraced the old woman.

Chiara had been working at the restaurant for a couple of months. One day, she saw Madame Dubois discarding a - mysterious-looking package into the outside bin.

"What was that?" Chiara asked when Madame Dubois returned to the kitchen.

"I put a couple of rats in the bin."

Chiara wrinkled her nose.

"We don't have any in our restaurant. I know how to keep them away," Madame Dubois said.

"What do you do?"Chiara asked.

"I got a strong rat poison. It works wonders. It takes care of pestilent things." Madame Dubois held out the rat poison and gave Chiara a knowing look.

"I keep it over here," she said, putting the small bottle with crossbones back in the cleaning supplies closet.

"*Cherié,* would you close the restaurant for me tonight? I have a doctor's appointment early tomorrow morning, and I don't want to be late."

"Sure. I'll clean up first and then I'll close. No problem."

"Thanks. You're sweet."

. . .

Uncertainty settled in Chiara's mind as she wondered about the woman Gino was seeing. Who was she? Was she younger than her? Was she beautiful?

Chiara needed to talk to someone. She phoned Sofia and invited her to have coffee at her place.

"Hey, sis," Chiara said when she opened the front door. She kissed Sofia on the cheek.

"Hey there, how're you doing?" Sofia asked coldly.

"Not too well, really," Chiara said while getting coffee ready.

"What's the matter?" A yawn escaped Sofia's mouth.

"It's about Gino."

"What about him?"

"Things aren't working between us. They haven't for a while." Chiara's chin trembled.

"What do you mean?" Sofia rubbed the back of her neck.

"I think he's seeing someone."

Sofia's heart skipped a beat. "Are you sure?"

"No, not a hundred percent."

"Then, don't worry about it. Why be concerned about something that maybe isn't true?" She tried to sound convincing.

"But he seems so distant, he doesn't wanna talk, doesn't wanna touch me. I don't think he loves me anymore." Chiara's voice broke.

"Come on, Chiara, don't be silly. We know guys are hard to understand. They live in their own world." Sofia swatted the air.

"Is Francesco good to you?"

"Yeah, sure, he's good. But I'm not in love with him anymore." Sofia offered a nonchalant shrug.

"Why not?"

"I'm just not. Period." She pressed her lips tight.

* * *

Sofia and Gino got to their favorite restaurant. After they ordered, she looked at him earnestly. "We can't keep going like this," she said, shifting in her chair.

"Why are you so edgy?"

"I think Chiara suspects something."

"Maybe she does, maybe she doesn't. We don't know for sure."

Sofia stared at the window for a long moment. "This uncertainty is killing me."

Gino caressed her hand and gazed into her eyes. "Let's enjoy our dinner, and we'll talk about this later."

Sofia nodded.

The next time Chiara did the laundry, she found another bill inside Steve's pants. This was the third one.

I think he leaves them on purpose. What a coward. He doesn't have the balls to tell me the truth.

She asked herself the same questions over and over.

Why? Where did I go wrong? Why can't he be honest with me?

The noise of the garage door closing interrupted her contemplation.

Gino slammed the kitchen door. "Traffic was a fucking nightmare." He threw his tool belt to the floor with a loud thud.

He's in a foul mood, but we have to talk, anyway.

After dinner, he sat on the porch to have a beer.

As determined as she pretended to be, Chiara said, "Steve, we need to talk."

"Could I have a frigging beer in peace, if you don't mind?"

"I need you to tell me about this," she shouted waving the bill in the air.

"Are you snooping around my shit?"

"I found this in your pants when doing your laundry."

"It's a restaurant bill, obviously."

"Well, tell me, who did you go with?"

"I took a client to close a deal. Do I have to explain my every move?"

He smashed the beer bottle against the wall, grabbed her by the arm, and threw her to the floor. "Leave me alone, bitch!" he yelled.

Trembling, Chiara stood up. Containing her rage, she demanded, "I know you're seeing someone. Tell me the truth. Who is she, bastard!"

"You want to know. You want to know her name?" His eyes bulged with fury. "It's Sofia. There, now you know!"

Time stopped tickling, and a feeling of betrayal overcame Chiara's body. Her scream of rage filled the entire house, following Gino as he headed to the garage.

The next day Chiara, went to work at the restaurant. Her ashen face, reddened eyes, and hunched shoulders alerted Madame Dubois.

"What happened to you, *cherié*? You look terrible."

Chiara slumped on a chair and stared at the ceiling for an overlong moment. Then, she answered. "It's about my husband."

Madame Dubois grimaced. "Tell me."

Chiara breathed deeply and said the words. "He's having an affair with my sister."

Madame Dubois turned away for a moment. Gaining composure she said, "I've heard that before. It doesn't make it any less hideous."

"How can I keep living?" Chiara asked, holding a sob.

"You'll find the way, *cherié*. Believe me, whatever happens in our lives, we always do."

Chiara chopped peppers, tomatoes, and herbs. She inhaled, savoring the rich aroma. *What a feast for the senses.*

Squaring her shoulders, she said, "It's time to take the

reins of my life." A sly smirk illuminated her face. "Sofia is coming over for dinner. I've prepared a flavorful dish for her and Gino."

While humming an old Tarantella, she added a sprinkle of a special ingredient from a small bottle.

"As Nonna Giulia used to say, the secret is in the sauce."

A NOVELLA

UNDER A WEEPING WILLOW

Timid rays of sun warmed up the crisp spring morning. A light breeze danced through vines that climbed up the walls of the white adobe house at the top of the hill, overlooking the valley below. Its terra-cotta roof tiles and blue-rimmed windows made it homey.

The house sat against a background of sheltering trees, and the Andes cordillera. Its awe-inspiring beauty served as a frame

work for the landscape. The mountain range stood imposing like an enormous protective guardian looking over the villagers.

An old weeping willow grew in the backyard. Its branches submerged in the clear waters of a small creek danced at the rhythm of a never-ending melody. Its waters fed the family orchard. From the garden, a fresh aroma of mint and lavender pervaded the air.

Alana left the house through a back door. Her long auburn braid ran down to her waist. The rhythmic movements of her hips and her tiny breasts hinted at womanhood. She carried a pail, walked to the pigpen, and opened the fence. The pigs rolled in the mud, but when they smelled food, they jostled toward her overflowing food-scrap bucket.

"Take it easy, gluttons. There's enough for all of you." She emptied the bucket into the pigs' large tub, wiped her hands on her frayed apron, and headed to the chicken coop, her wicker basket on hand.

"Sorry girls, I need to get some eggs first. Then I'll feed you." She giggled. The chicken's deafening clucking didn't bother her. After Alana finished feeding them, she returned to the house. The main room served as a kitchen, eating area, and family room. A large wood-burning stove stood at its centre. Bunches of garlic and other herbs hung from the rafters. A wicker basket full of potatoes sat in a corner.

"I'm done with my chores, Mama. I've got seven eggs." She set the wicker basket on the long wooden table.

"Thank you, amor. Go, wash your hands, and get your books ready for school. We'll wait for your brothers to have breakfast. They went to the well to get water."

Margot, her mother, stood by the wood stove stirring a boiling pot of oatmeal.

Living in the 1950s, in an impoverished country town was a hard endeavour, but Margot was a strong-willed woman with a tireless spirit whose short stature and fragile appearance were deceiving. On the side of her chest, a deep brown hair, hanging in a tidy braid, followed the rhythm of her breathing. Married at fifteen, Margot had dedicated her life to raising a family with little money and a lot of hard work.

As usual when cooking she hummed a melody.

"I like it when you sing, Mama."

"I wasn't singing, just humming."

"I like your humming, too."Alana paused before asking, "Mama, are you happy?"

"What kind of question is that?"

"A simple one."

"Yes, I'm happy."

"Why"?

"I'm happy because there is food on the table and we have a roof over our heads. But mostly I'm happy because I have good children. Especially you, amor."

Alana's big brown eyes became watery. A wave of love swept over her. She hugged her mother, "I love you too, mucho."

Mama seems happy, most of the time. It must be hard for her to look after all of us, especially with Papa gone. I'm old enough to see it. I wonder why Papa isn't home.

* * *

Margot did the best she could to look after her family. Not having her husband around was hard but she decided not to let his absence bring her down.

When summer arrived, the village came alive with the harvesting season. Some farmers hired temporary workers to help with the gathering of crops. They were men that travel from place to place working from sunup to sundown, usually with minimal payment.

Observing these workers around, sadness and a sense of empathy came over Margot. She was glad to provide some relief from the heat by offering fresh water when required.

When handing a glass of water to a worker, something called her attention. Glinting in the sun, green and pale blue rosary beads hang from his pants pockets.

This man may not have much, but he has his faith, Margot thought.

* * *

Alana, ten-year-old Paco, and seven-year-old Marcia walked to school together. Each carried a small handmade burlap sack which contained a pencil, a notebook, and a piece of fruit or bread. Paco wore pants and a loose top made of coarse fabric, while the girls wore faded percale dresses.

They went through fields and meadows, goofing around, running, or walking. It took them almost an hour to get to school.

"Hurry up you two, we aren't there yet," Alana said.

They marched down the pathway bordered by berry bushes. "I want to pick some berries. Just a few, please Alana, please," her little sister begged.

"No. We can't be late for school."

"You're so mean." Marcia mocked a pout.

When her siblings behaved and walked quietly, Alana enjoyed losing herself in her thoughts. *Someday I'd like to become a teacher. Maybe get married and have a family. I like going to school; it's fun. We have a good teacher. Don Manuel is kind to us and so good-looking. My heart flutters when he's nearby.*

Because they were late for classes, Alana took a shortcut, a leafy side path running along the creek seemed like a quicker route.

A sudden noise from behind a bush took her utterly by surprise. "Who's there?" Alana's voice quivered. A shudder rippled through her body. Her muscles tensed and her posture became rigid. A cold shiver went down her spine.The shadow jumped from nowhere and grabbed her. Gasping for air and before the attacker covered her mouth, she managed to shout; "Run home kids, run!"

The terrified children ran down the path, crying and screaming, "Mama, Mama!"

Alana tried to release herself from the strong arms that imprisoned her from behind. With the sound of her heartbeat thrashing in her ears, she fought with all her might, but her efforts were useless against the strength of her aggressor. Suddenly, the attacker kicked the back of her leg and she fell to the ground. A sharp blow to the back of her head was the last thing she remembered as blackness engulfed her.

. . .

When the children arrived home, they couldn't utter a word. Their faces, contorted by fear, spoke of something terrifying.

"Where is she, where is she?" Margot shouted. She shook Paco's shoulders in despair. Her eyes were wide open and her whole body trembled. The children didn't see Alana's attacker, so they couldn't describe him to their mother.

Following Paco, Margot ran like a madwoman, her heart galloping. They found Alana unconscious, lying under a bush. The girl's messy hair and torn dress broke Margot's heart.

"Baby, baby!" She patted Alana's face.

No answer.

She carried her daughter home, the boy trotting behind her. She asked Paco to take care of Marcia and put Alana to bed.

"Mama, Mama." A half-awake Alana said.

"Hush, hush, amor. Go to sleep."

Margot caressed her daughter's face and gently covered her eyes with her hand, humming a lullaby until Alana went to sleep.

What happened to my girl? Should I go to the police? What for? They wouldn't listen to a poor country woman. Oh, Pedro, where are you when I need you the most? Why did you leave us?

After a sleepless night, she left the house.

* * *

Margot needed to talk to Eulalia, the local medicine woman. Everybody called her la curandera, the village's witch. People said she made a pact with Satan to save her child's life but the little girl died anyway. Perhaps those were only rumours. Some people believed she was evil, but others thought of her as a good witch.

Everyone knew the old woman did extraordinary things. The witch moved objects without touching them, predicted the future, made magic potions and talked to ghosts.

She delivered babies, alive or dead. She also helped the dying to cross to the

other side.

Maybe she could help Margot protect her daughter.

At sunset, Margot arrived at the witch's hut. The hues and shades of twilight painted the sky and an eerie feeling overwhelmed her. The hut was constructed with scrap wood, cardboard, and some pieces of broken bricks. Two small windows covered with clear plastic let scant light in. She knocked on the flimsy door. "Are you home, Eulalia?"

An elderly woman wearing a ragged skirt and a faded blouse opened the door. Her toothless smile greeted Margot. Draped over her shoulders, an old black shawl hung down to the floor. Wrinkles from forehead to neck showed the passing of years, yet she looked clean and her breath smelled of cinnamon. Curious eyes deep in their sockets observed the visitor.

"Hello, there. Come in," she said.

Margot entered the room. The surroundings looked

ghostly in the dim light. A wobbly round table and a couple of straw-bottomed chairs stood at the center of the room. Some wooden planks arranged against the wall and separated by a few bricks served as improvised pieces of furniture. The shelves held various objects, an odd-looking mirror, a small statue of the Virgin Mary, kitchenware, a wooden box, a candle in its holder, and an animal skull. Branches of dry herbs and twigs hung from the low ceiling.

An uneasy feeling overtook Margot."I hope I didn't disturb you."

"Not at all. At my age, time drags on. I like to receive visitors. Would you like some water? I ran out of tea," she said.

"No, thanks."

"Take a seat," Eulalia said, pointing to the other chair. The old woman observed the visitor closely. Her inquisitive stare made Margot nervous. "Fine. Tell me, what can I do for you?"

Margot sat at the edge of the chair. She closed her eyes and took a calming breath. "I need your help. I don't have any money, but I could bring you a chicken, corn, and potatoes."

"Thank you. I'm listening."

Margot rubbed her hands on the side of her dress." I need a magic potion for my daughter."

Eulalia squinted. "What is her problem?"

Margot's chin quavered. "I want Alana to forget what happened to her. She was assaulted today on her way to school." She swallowed and wiped a tear. "I'm not sure what happened, but I found her unconscious. Her dress was bloody. Please, help me."

The witch gazed at Margot with empathy. "I'll help you, but you shouldn't talk to anyone about what I'm going to do." She stood, grabbed a dried root from a box on the shelf and gave it to Margot. "Boil this, make a tea and give it to your daughter."

Margot held the root with shaking hands. "Thanks," she said.

"Before you go, understand this. The mind is an obscure thing. We can't ever be sure of its mysteries."

Margot looked puzzled. "What do you mean?"

The old woman didn't reply.

Night arrived at the small country town. As Margot strode back home, a moonless night darkened the stars.

* * *

When Alana opened her eyes, her head spun. A bitter taste lingered in her mouth. In her ears, a hundred drums beat uncontrollably.

"Mama, where are you?" Her voice quivered.

Margot held her daughter's hand. "I'm here, amor. Try to sleep. I gave you something to help you rest."

"What happened, Mama?"

"Go to sleep, baby, sleep," she whispered.

Alana's eyes grew heavier, her mind couldn't focus on her surroundings.

While her daughter slept, Margot stroked her rosary beads and prayed.

In her mother's bed and in a fetal position, Alana dreamed. In her dream, she stood at the top of a mountain, enjoying a magnificent view of a valley. She closed her eyes, and let the sun's rays caress her face. Still dreaming, suddenly, the sky went dark, a cold breeze made her shiver and a loud sound startled her. For a terrifying second, she didn't know what was happening. An enormous black bird loomed above her head, lifting her into the sky. Her heart thumped in her chest, jaw clenched and a feeling of fear overwhelmed her.

After flying higher and higher, the ferocious bird let her go into the emptiness. A guttural sound escaped her mouth. She opened her eyes. Holding back a cry, she covered her mouth with both hands.

She sprang from her bed and shouted, "Mama, Mama!" Her glance darted around the room. As she rubbed her temples, a foggy cloud hung over her head.

"Calm down, amor, you might still feel dizzy from the medicine I gave you."

"What was that for?"

"It was a medicine to help you feel better."

"What happened to me?"

An empty feeling in the pit of her stomach took over Margot. "I don't know. I think you fainted or maybe you tripped over a rock and hit your head. I'm not sure."

Alana frowned. "What?"

"Yesterday, shortly after you and the children left for school, they came back to the house running and shouting for me. They told me you were hurt."

"Oh, I don't remember any of that."

"When I ran to your side, you were unconscious, with a large bump on your head."

"I have no idea what you're talking about." She touched the back of her head. "It's a big bump. I can feel it." Then, she rubbed her lower abdomen."Mama, it also hurts down there, why?"

Margot's face turned ashen. "I think you could be having your first bleed, baby. When it happens some women's private parts get quite sore, but it will pass."

"I hope so."

"I want you to rest, amor."A worried look settled on Margot's face.

Alana squeezed her hands tight."I don't want to rest, I want to remember what happened to me. Don't you understand?" She pounded a fist against the pillow.

"What for? You are well now. In a couple of days, you'll go back to school, and all will be fine, as always."

Alana raised her voice. "I'm not a child anymore. I'll turn fourteen next month. I need to know what happened to me."

"Amor, let it go." She caressed Alana's face. "I need to make tomorrow's bread. I'll be in the kitchen." She pulled up her daughter's blanket to keep her warm.

Alana let out a long sigh of frustration and closed her eyes.

While in the kitchen, Margot wrestled with feelings of guilt about being untruthful to her daughter. *I can't tell Alana what happened. It'd hurt her deeply. My duty as a mother is to protect my child. Then, why do I feel so bad? Am I doing the right thing?*

Night settled on the adobe house at the top of the hill. Shadows danced on the bedroom walls, reflecting the light from the bedside table's oil lamp.

Through the window, Alana gazed toward the moonless sky and searched for distant stars. For a while, she wondered what had happened. Somehow, her body sensed something bad took place, but what? Not finding any answers, she went to bed and curled up by Marcia's warm body. Sleep didn't come easily.

* * *

After a few days, Alana felt well enough to return to school. As usual, when walking, Marcia hummed a lullaby and held hands with her older sister.

"Sweetie, I need to ask you something. What happened to me the other day when we walked to school?" Alana asked.

"Mama said, we are not allowed to tell you."

"Why not?

"I don't know, but Mama said so." The girl shrugged her shoulders.

Alana pressed her sister to tell her the truth , but Marcia remained quiet.

Alana pursed her lips in thought.

A radiant sun illuminated the valley when the children arrived at their destination. Two rooms, an office, and an outhouse made up the rural school. About a dozen students shared the main classroom.

Children of different ages sat in an orderly fashion. The younger ones, grades one, two, and three sat at the front. The higher grades sat at the back. In the smaller room students had activities such as crafts and painting.

A man stood in front of the class. Tall and thin, Manuel Garcia seemed too young to be a teacher. A lock of hair fell over his forehead. He wore old trousers and a faded striped shirt. His affable smile made the students feel welcome. "Good morning children."

"Good morning teacher," they stood and answered in unison.

Manuel attended to each student, checked homework, and assigned new tasks. As he approached Alana's desk, he observed her demeanour. She sat quietly at her desk, note-book unopened. Idly, she tapped her pencil on her chin, while looking toward the classroom window. Wiping a tear with the back of her hand, she let out a sigh.

"You seem distracted this morning. Are you feeling well?" He crouched beside her desk.

She didn't reply.

He insisted, "If you have a problem, you know you can talk to me. I'm your teacher and I care about you."

She looked up at him."I don't want to talk about it."

"Alana, do you trust me?"

"Si."

"Tell me. What is the problem?"

"I don't know how to explain it."

"Try me."

"Something weird happened to me the other day." She folded her arms across her chest.

"What do you mean?"

"When coming to school, I think something bad happened, but I can't remember what." Her voice broke and she dabbed a tear.

"Don't cry. We'll talk about it later, okay?"

She nodded.

After the school day, Manuel sat pensively at his desk and pondered about Alana's conversation.

* * *

Black towering clouds threatened the sky when Manuel got to Alana's home. A couple of dogs announced his arrival before he opened the wooden fence.

Margot came outside, drying her hands on her apron. "Hello, Don Manuel. Come in."

"Thank you."

"Have a seat." Margot offered him a straw-bottomed chair. She grabbed another chair and sat facing him.

"May I offer you some tea?" she asked.

"No, thanks."

"There is something you need to talk about?"

The rain started, followed by a gusty wind knocking at the windows. Manuel cleared his throat. "Yes. It's about Alana."

"What about her?"

"She hasn't been herself lately. Showed no interest in her schoolwork and cried in class." He paused for a moment. "She told me something happened to her on her way to school the other day, but she couldn't remember what it was. That's quite unusual." He noticed Margot's rapid blinking.

"She is a grown-up child, you know. Sometimes they are a bit hard to understand." Margot twisted her long braid aimlessly.

"I don't think this has to do with teen behaviour." He gazed at her intently.

Margot twisted her fingers, her palms sweating. "Promise me, Don Manuel, you won't talk to anyone about what I'm about to tell you."

"I promise."

"A couple of days ago, while I was working in the orchard, Paco and Marcia came running up the hill. They screamed for me." She paused to gain some composure.

Outside a deluge unfolded and rain splattered all over the windows.

Margot went on. "The children told me Alana was hurt. They said she was on the road to school near the creek. I ran faster than the wind followed by Paco. When we got there, Alana lay on the ground."

Mouth agape, Manuel scanned Margot's face. "Please, keep going," he said.

"I knelt beside her. She was almost unconscious. When I saw her ripped dress, her bloody legs, and her messy hair, I knew what had happened to my girl." She covered her mouth with a hand to stifle a sob.

Manuel's eyes bulged. "What did you do?

"I carried her home, cleaned her up, and put her to bed. Then, I went to see Eulalia."

"La curandera, la bruja?" Manuel asked in disbelief.

"Don't call her that. She isn't a bad witch as some people think. She's a medicine woman, a healer, an old wise person who knows a lot about everything and helps people."

"I don't care what you called her. She practices witchcraft. That could be dangerous."

"Eulalia gave me a special root to prepare a beverage. She said it'll erase from Alana's mind all memory of what happened. I gave it to her. So far, it has worked. What else could I have done?" Her harsh stare didn't intimidate Manuel.

He looked at her straight. "You could have gone to the police to report the incident."

"Do you think they'd truly care about a poor country-woman with this type of complaint? The police know it happens often, whether you believe it or not."

"Margot, forgive me, but, I think Alana should know the truth."

"What? Are you out of your mind?"

"It's not fair to keep her in the dark," he insisted.

"Do you want to talk about fairness? My fourteen-year-old girl suffered an assault. Was that fair?"

Manuel kept silent.

"You don't understand. You're not a parent and have no idea what it means to be responsible for a child's well-being. I want you to leave," she said.

"Margot, let's keep talking."

"No. Please, leave." She walked to the door and opened it.

He stood and left.

You are wrong, Margot. I do have someone to care for, Manuel thought as he walked into the torrent of rain.

* * *

The sun had set when Manuel got home. Three rooms made up his house-the large main one and two small bedrooms. The place looked modest and clean while minimal furniture and few possessions spoke of hard times.

Fernando, Manuel's younger brother, was nine when the father left the family. Their mother took her younger son and went back to live with her parents in another town, while Manuel attended teaching school. But since his mother passing a few months ago, it was his responsibility to look after his mentally-challenged brother.

Manuel made his way to Fernando's bedroom. He found him lying on his bed, arms crossed over his chest, his brow furrowed.

"Why are you so late? I was scared," Fernando said.

"Sorry, but I had to go to a parent's home to talk about a student." Manuel sat by the side of the bed and ruffled his brother's hair. "There is no reason to be scared."

Fernando stood, leaned over and hugged his brother. He towered over Manuel. He was a hefty teenager with dark curls, a friendly smile and the intellectual development of a much younger boy. He refused to go to school and mingled with other children because he was timid and introverted. He sensed he was different. So, Manuel home-schooled him. With great effort, the boy learned to write but he read poorly.

With the back of his hand, Fernando dabbed away a small drool running down from the corner of his mouth. "I'm hungry," he said.

"Good. We'll eat soon."

When Manuel was at work, his brother looked after the orchard, fed the animals, and wandered the fields.

At dinner, he noted his brother didn't eat much."Are you sick? Most of the time you devour your food."

"I wasn't hungry, after all." He looked away.

Later on, the two sat by the fire. Fernando bounced his knee while rubbing his cheek.

Manuel sensed his brother's state of mind. "You seem nervous, something happened?"

Fernando stuttered. "Hum...no, I don't think so."

Manuel insisted. "I know you want to tell me something. Don't be shy. Talk to me."

"I...I like a girl, she is so pretty, maybe I'm in love... I don't know..." He stumbled

over his words.

Trying to conceal his surprise, Manuel said, "That's good, I guess." He wished her mother was around; he didn't find the words for this occasion."Tell me more."

"I tried to kiss her, but she slapped my face. She doesn't like me."

"Who is this girl?"

"Alana."

Manuel's mind whirled and his heart accelerated. He stood and faced his brother,

"What happened? Answer me. What did you do to her?" Manuel's eyes widened.

"I told you already. I wanted to kiss her, but she got scared, slapped me and

pushed me away. So, I left."

"Are you sure?" He grabbed his brother's arm.

"Yes, I'm sure. You're hurting me!" Fernando jerked his arm away.

Manuel shot him a stare, "You shouldn't have done that.

Don't you ever kiss a girl without her consent. Promise me you won't do it again."

Fernando lowered his gaze, "I promise," he said. "Should I ask her to forgive me?"

"No, don't do it," Manuel raised his voice.

"Why not?" Fernando scanned his brother's face for an explanation.

Manuel swallowed hard, "I don't want you to upset her again."

The boy didn't reply. He was taught to apologize when behaving badly. It was strange his brother didn't want him to.

Manuel let out a groan and slumped on a chair.

That night, in bed, he ruminated about the whole affair. Was Fernando telling the truth? Was he capable of attacking Alana? No, he didn't think his brother would do something like that.

The first light of dawn broke in the unlit sky, but Manuel's heart remained in darkness.

* * *

The following morning, a Sunday, there was no school. When Manuel got up. Fernando had set the table for breakfast. They ate in silence.

After they finished, the boy stood and said, "I'm going to work in the orchard. It's time to pitch apples."

Manuel hardly touched his food. A wave of dread washed over him. "No, sit. We have to talk."

"About what?" Fernando twisted his fingers.

"About Alana. Listen, I don't want you to talk to anyone about what happened to her. Is that clear?"

Fernando stared at the floor. "Yes."

"When I'm working, I don't want you to wander the fields. You hear me?"

"What am I supposed to do?"

"You'll work in the orchard and look after the animals. I'll also give you school work." Manuel took his brother's face with both hands. "If you don't obey me, I'll punish you. I'm not kidding."

"I'll be good. Every day," the boy said.

* * *

Margot repeated a sentence in her head over and over. "Life must go on." And it did, until a couple of months later.

She was cooking when Alana entered the kitchen. "How are you, love?" Margot said.

"Fine, I guess. But, I need to ask you something."

"Go ahead."

"I haven't had my monthly bleeding. And I feel weird. Is that normal?"

Margot felt the blood drain from her face. Her lips quivered.

"Mama, you feel well? You don't look too good."

"I'm fine."

Alana touched her mother's hand. "Maybe you should rest."

"No, I don't need to rest. Let's talk about your monthly bleeding or the lack of it."

"I told you already, I'm not bleeding anymore. Also, my breasts feel kind of

tender." Alana placed her hands on her chest.

"You know amor, women's bodies are not easy to understand. When you are very young, your body is learning to do things right," Margot said.

"What do you mean?" Alana wrinkled her forehead.

"Well, some women may have a bleed twice a month or not have one for a month or so. We're all different."

"Umm, I see. But, what about my breasts?"

"I've seen you running around without your bra. Your bust is growing and you need to wear it. Maybe that's the reason your breasts feel a bit sore."

"Good. I'm happy we talked." She kissed her mother on the cheek and skipped out of the room.

Margot closed her eyes and tried to clear her mind. *Oh, God, what would happen if Alana is pregnant? She isn't even aware of the attack. I have to protect her, but how?*

* * *

บริษัท รถรุ่งเรือง จำกัด

ROONG REUANG COACH CO.,LTD

email : rrc_bus@hotmail.com

เลขตั๋ว 11-022909-66

วันที่ 19/11/2566

ชื่อ
NAME

type 1

สถานี เส้นทางพัทยา เอกมัย
FORM Pattaya - Ekamai(BANGKOK)

เวลาออก ~~11:40~~ เบอร์รถ 48-2
TIME [11:40 BUS NO

เลขที่นั่ง 7 ราคา 131
SEAT NO PRICE

นส ชฎาพร ลาดำ (ผู้โดยสาร/PASSENGER)

บริษัท รถรุ่งเรือง จำกัด

ROONG REUANG COACH CO.,LTD

email : rrc_bus@hotmail.com

เลขตั๋ว 11-022910-66

วันที่ 19/11/2566

ชื่อ
NAME

type 1

สถานี เส้นทางพัทยา-เอกมัย
FORM Pattaya - Ekamai(BANGKOK)

เวลาออก 11:40
TIME [11:40

เบอร์รถ 48-2
BUS NO

เลขที่นั่ง 8
SEAT NO

ราคา 131
PRICE

นส ชฎาพร ลาดำ (ผู้โดยสาร/PASSENGER)

Gray clouds loomed in the sky when Margot got to the medicine woman's hut. A chilly breeze made her shiver. She knocked on the door and waited.

Eulalia's toothless smile greeted her. "Hello, Margot, it's nice to see you again. Come in. It's getting cold."

Margot carried a large bag and placed it at the old woman's feet. "I brought you fresh onions."

"Thanks. Tell me what I can do for you." She rearranged her worn-out black shawl over her shoulders.

Margot cleared her voice. "My daughter hasn't bled in about two months."

"Do you think she is with child?" Eulalia squinted.

"I'm afraid so."

"What do you want me to do?"

Margot swallowed. "I need something to make her bleed."

The old woman rubbed her palms. When she spoke, her voice was dark and foreboding. "First, I must warn you. We can't change destiny. What's written in the stars is final. I can only help you to better your chances."

"I don't understand."

"I could give you something to help your daughter bleed. After drinking the potion, most women do. But, some don't. I don't know why."

Eulalia stood, her old bones creaking. She grabbed a burlap bag and put it on the table. Her knotted fingers rummaged through its contents.

Finally, she took out a piece of root and gave it to Margot.

"Boil this and give it to your daughter. She must drink the tea during a full moon." She added, "You better pray."

Margot held the root with shaking hands, hoping that Eulalia's medicine would work its magic.

* * *

Alana and the children strolled back from school. They ran and picked wild blackberries from the bushes along the road. Their smeared faces and black smiles glowed under the sun. Alana walked behind them.

"Please, Alana, I have to wash my face. I feel sticky." little Marcia begged.

"Fine, but hurry up. Mama is waiting for us."

While her sister washed her face by the creekside, Alana carefully scanned her surroundings. The splatter of water running through the pebbles and the rushing sound of the breeze through the nearby trees made her heart pound. Something about the place made her tremble. Her eyes darted right and left. Nobody was around.

"I'm ready," Marcia said as she dried her hands on her skirt.

Alana held her sister's hand and plodded home followed by Paco. Her heart couldn't stop throbbing.

* * *

Swaths of wheat across the meadow painted hues of red and yellow on the skyline. The aroma of early spring spread through the air as Margot harvested corn on the field. With the back of her hand, she dried pearly drops of perspiration on her forehead. Her tongue felt dry; she needed to quench her thirst.

She glanced at the weeping willow at the back of the patio. Its lower branches floating in the creek's water brought to mind special memories. She was fifteen when Pedro kissed her for the first time under a willow. It seemed like it happened a lifetime ago. After taking a deep breath, she closed her eyes. Her heart ached for her husband. She needed him home.

Before entering the house, Margot looked at the road that wound down to the valley. A large silhouette on a horse was too far away to distinguish. She squinted, and her hand flew to her brow.

As the figure approached, her vision cleared. Her heart skipped a beat. She mouthed a name, *Pedro*. Butterflies danced in her stomach as he got closer.

The tall man wore his light brown hair down to the shoulders. An unkempt beard encircled his sad face. He looked haggard. Pedro got off the horse and without saying a word, he hugged her. His downcasted expression touched Margot's heart. She melted in his arms and sobbed quietly.

After a couple of minutes, she took a big breath. "I can't believe it's you."

He could hardly speak. "It's me."

"I'm glad you remembered you have a family. Come inside. We'll talk later," she said.

They entered the house together. Pedro's sad blue eyes scanned the room, recognizing every object; the large wooden table, the stove, the wicker chaise, and the bottom-straw chairs.

He kept every item engraved in his memory. Nothing had changed since the day he left. Heart pounding, Pedro sat by the table and buried his head in his hands. An uncontrollable torrent of silent tears ran down his cheeks.

Margot squeezed his shoulder gently. "Let it all out. You'll feel better."

When the children arrived from school and saw Pedro's horse, they ran inside

shouting and jumping. Their eyes lit up with glee, as they pushed each other to get to their father first, "Papa, Papa," they shouted.

Pedro hugged them; his heart full of joy. Gazing at his children through misty eyes, he realized how much he had missed them.

"Papi, Papi, are you staying?" Little Marcia asked.

"Don't you ever go away," Paco pleaded.

"Hola, Papa," said Alana from a distance.

"Could I have a hug?" he asked her.

She walked toward her father and let him hug her.

"Everybody, wash your hands. We are ready to eat." Margot said, trying to contain her emotions.

After dinner, the children went to bed. Margot cleared

the dishes and fidgeted with menial tasks. She observed Pedro's tired expression. Dark shadows encircled his eyes. A wave of sympathy enveloped her.

Fighting to keep her feelings aside, she said, "I'm tired, I'm going to bed." Without giving Pedro a chance to reply, she added, "You could sleep in the barn tonight."

Pedro's eyes begged. "Please, could we talk for a minute?"

"I said I'm tired. We'll talk tomorrow." Before leaving the room she handed him a blanket. "This should keep you warm."

"Thank you," he said.

She sensed his eyes following her leaving.

* * *

Back in her bed, Margot toyed with her wedding band twisting it around her finger aimlessly. She thought about what Pedro had done. He left the family home two months ago for the town's market without giving an explanation. He simply hadn't come back. Desperation invaded Margot's soul when her husband disappeared.

She searched for Pedro everywhere, at the district hospital, and the local jail, but to no avail. When she realized her husband wasn't coming back, she did what she had to. She kept going. She had kids to feed, animals to look after, and tears to hide.

Margot dreamed about having Pedro back home for so

long and now she didn't know how to feel. But he was her husband, the father of her children. Wasn't that enough?

At the barn, Pedro threw the blanket over loose hay and used his old burlap sack as an improvised pillow. His eyes darted around the old barn he had built a long time ago. Fifteen years to be exact, the length of their marriage.

He thought of Margot as the shy girl he had kissed for the first time under the weeping willow, by the old creek. His mind wondered if that had happened to him or to someone else. He tossed and turned until dawn.

* * *

Glimmering rays of sun painted the sky as Pedro walked to the well. The fresh countryside breeze invigorated him. He carried two pails he found in the barn and stood in front of the kitchen door, too hesitant to knock. Through the window, Margot saw him coming. Her heart couldn't stop dancing.

She opened the door. "Good morning. I'm glad you got water."

"Good morning," he said and placed the pails by the side of the stove.

The children were having breakfast and they got up to hug their father. All except for Alana.

"How do you like your school, children?" he asked as he freed himself from Marcia's tight embrace.

"I know how to write my name, Papi," the little one said.

"We are doing good, Papa," his son answered.

"What about you, Alana?" He glanced at his oldest daughter.

She looked at the floor, her nails digging into her palms. "I'm fine," She added, "Hurry up kids, we are getting late."

After the children left, Margot served him a portion of porridge and a piece of bread.

"That's all we have. I gave the children milk and they have eggs on Sundays. The rest we sell." Her upper lip curled in disdain.

"Thanks," he said and emptied his plate. After he finished, he asked, "Could we

talk?"

Margot crumpled her apron. She sat facing Pedro." Yes, I think we have to."

"I don't know where to start."

"What about telling me why you left home without saying a word? You don't know what I've been through, looking for you, hoping you were alive."

He looked at her, his eyes pleading for forgiveness. Unable to find the right words, he kept silent.

"I'm waiting for an explanation." Margot crossed her arms over her chest, her

right foot tapping the floor. She could see the shame on his face.

His cheeks burned and his shoulders hunched. "I was a selfish coward," he said.

"Yes, you were. Tell me what happened. Why did you leave?"

Pedro moved away from the table, walked towards the window, and gazed at the old willow. "I'll start at the beginning. Do you remember when the circus came to town last summer? I met someone there. A trapeze artist."

Margot's unrelenting stare wasn't much of an encouragement for Pedro to continue, but he did.

"I was crazy about her and when she asked me to follow her with the circus, I did." He

dropped his head to his chin.

"I can't believe what I'm hearing." Margot's hands flew to her chest, and she shook her head.

"I worked at the circus doing whatever they wanted me to do, to be close to her. That

woman bewitched me," He swallowed hard. "I'm so sorry for what I've done. Maybe one day you could forgive me."

"You are sorry? You have no idea what I've been through, with the kids, without

any money. Our savings lasted me a couple of weeks. After that, we survived by selling eggs, milk, cream, butter, veggies from the garden, and the charity of our neighbours." She made an effort to hold her tears. "What happened to your trapeze artist?"

"She met someone else and got rid of me."

Margot tightened her hands into fists. "So, that's the reason you're back."

"No, it's not. She was a mistake. I missed you and the children."

"Why am I supposed to believe you?"

"Because it's the truth. This place needs a man and the children need a father."

"You should've thought about your family before running after that wicked

woman."

He slipped his hands into the pockets of his old pants. "What can I do to regain your trust?"

"Be a man. Being one is more than fathering children. You need to be responsible for

your family."

"I'll be one if you give me a chance. May I come back here?"

She drew a breath and released it. "You can sleep in the house but not in my bedroom. I have work to do in the orchard. Are you coming?"

Pedro followed her.

* * *

From dusk to dawn Pedro tried to figure out a way to get close to Margot's heart. He told her he felt repentant and remorseful for what he had done. He admitted that it was shameful to leave his family to chase another woman.

Pedro kept working in the orchard, milking cows and

feeding animals. Every day was similar to the previous one, which made his life devoid of joy.

The young children, happy to have their father home, came running home from school every day shouting at the top of their lungs: "Papi, Papi."

Alana kept avoiding her father. Her contact with him was minimal, a cold embrace before going to school because Margot insisted, and another one at bedtime. She couldn't stand to be near him. His presence soured her mood.

Concerned about Alana's attitude toward her father, Margot asked her, "What's wrong with you?"

"Nothing. Why?"

"Don't play games with me. You hardly talk to your father and I don't like the way you look at him."

"What do you want me to do?" She rolled her eyes.

"Try to be more understanding. I know he behaved badly, but he's home now and he's repentant."

"If you want to have him back, that's your choice. But you can't make me love him again."

"Amor, life will teach you to forgive not once, but many times. We all make mistakes. Maybe you're too young to understand."

As an answer, Alana clenched her teeth. After a few seconds, she asked, "May I go now?"

Margot sat by the kitchen table. How could she ask her daughter to pardon Pedro when she herself was unable to find forgiveness in her heart? As a mother, she had to think of her children first. They needed Pedro to survive, it was that simple. She rested her head on her forearms and quietly cried.

Pedro walked in.

He hand caressed her hair. "I'm so sorry for the pain I'm causing you. I wish I could take it away."

He sat by her side and gently lifted Margot's chin kissing her cheeks, savouring the salty taste of her tears. Working his way to her mouth, he kissed her gently. She didn't reject his kiss but didn't part her lips either. After Pedro's insistence, she gave in. It was a long passionate kiss.

A warm feeling traveled into her loins. His hand found its way to her chest and under her blouse, he discovered her erect nipples. His rough palm stroked them so gently. She couldn't stop a soft moan. It had been so long since they'd been together. A sudden urgency invaded every fibre of her being.

Margot stood and hugged him. He rubbed his body against hers, and she felt him ready. She grabbed Pedro's hand and they walked to her bedroom. They were hungry for each other.

After lovemaking, Margot's head rested in the hollow of his arm. She rejoiced in his familiar scent, a mixture of freshly harvested wheat and ripe fruit.

All of those aromas permeated his skin, making her senses come alive. Sleep came easily for them.

When Pedro woke, he heard Margot getting the children ready for school. She did her chores absent-mindedly and let her thoughts wander. *I still love him, in spite of him being a bad husband. But love won't be enough. He needs to gain my trust.*

After breakfast, Margot sat by Pedro's side. She looked serious.

"What's the matter?" he asked.

"I need to talk to you about Alana."

" What about her?"

Margot told him everything. She talked about Alana's assault, her visits to Eulalia's hut, the potions the medicine woman gave her, and the possibility of Alana's pregnancy.

Pedro made an effort to focus on what she said. It seemed he was hearing someone else's tragic family story. Not his. Bewilderment, disbelief, and rage made him tremble. Against his best efforts, his blue eyes welled up. Holding his head with both hands, he muttered, "This is all my fault. I wasn't here to protect my family."

Margot touched his hand. "Nobody could've prevented the assault. It just happened."

"But you had to go through all of this on your own. I'm a piece of shit. But I'll make it up to you. I'll find the bastard and I'll kill him."

"Don't say that. We don't know who he was."

"I said I'll find him! "

"What would we do if you go to jail? Think about it."

"What are we supposed to do, then?" he asked.

"Alana had the potion Eulalia gave me. Now we wait and pray. That's all we can do."

* * *

It had been several days since Alana drank the potion Margot gave her. The last days of autumn carried with them the brown, terra-cotta and orange shades of the season. The chilled morning breeze made the yellow leaves dance.

Alana wore her heavy poncho to keep warm when going to the well. The sun had set on the horizon as she dawdled toward the house holding a pail in each hand.

In an instant, sharp pain stopped her in her tracks. It felt like a knife perforating her lower belly, dropping her drop to her knees. The pails went flying. She shouted for her mother before she fainted.

Margot ran to her daughter, knelt by her side, and held the girl's face.

"Amor! What happened?" Margot's heart pounded and her chin quivered. She stared at her daughter's pale face looking for an answer.

Alana lay on the ground, white-lipped and unconscious. Margot carried her to the house and put her down on a wicker chaise. She got a few cushions, lifted Alana's feet up, and shook her daughter's shoulders gently.

"Baby, wake up, I'm here."

After a few minutes, a faint cry escaped Alana's mouth. Her hands flew to her lower belly. "It hurts, it hurts."

"What hurts? Where does it hurt, baby?"

"Down there, Mama."

Margot softly touched Alana's lower abdomen.

Pain disfigured Alana's face."It hurts."

Margot kissed her daughter's forehead. "I'll get a hot water bottle for your belly. That'll ease the pain a little."

"Thanks, Mama." A light pink colour started to return to her face.

When Margot lifted her daughter's poncho, she realized the extent of Alana's bleeding. She swallowed hard, mouthed "my God"and covered Alana."Amor, I think your period is back. That's good, I'll clean you up, try to sleep. You'll feel better."

* * *

Pedro returned from the town's market. His horse-drawn carriage felt light; he had sold everything his family harvested. He bought the groceries Margot asked for. It was a good day's work.

When Pedro entered the kitchen, Margot's anxious look alerted him.

"What happened?"

"Alana's sick. She is bleeding."

"Is she hurt"

"She is not hurt, but she's bleeding from...down there. You're a man, you don't get it."

"How can I help?"

" Go and get Eulalia. Hurry up!"

He rushed to his horse, his mind in turmoil. The frenzied horse galloped through forests and meadows. The wind blew Pedro's hair and his breathing became heavy. His brain

imagined every sinister scenario.

When Pedro arrived at Eulalia's place, his heart throbbed wildly in his chest. He got off

his horse, ran to the hut, and banged its door. The old woman's voice came through the entrance.

"Who is there?"

"It's Pedro. Please, open up."

"It's dark already. Go home."

"Please, we need you. Alana is very sick."

Eulalia peeked through the hut's only window, "What did you say? My hearing isn't too good these days."

"You need to see Alana. She's bleeding. Please, come with me."

"Ah, you better come back in the morning. I'll see her then."

"No, tomorrow my daughter could be dead. We need you now."

Not wanting to get up from her warm bed, Eulalia dragged her feet and opened the door.

"People shouldn't get sick at this time of night, for God's sake. What happened to her?"

"I'm not sure. Women's things, my wife said. Please, we need to hurry up."

. . .

Eulalia held on tightly to Pedro's waist while they rode. Drizzle soaked her hair. Despite her poncho, the cold chilled her old bones and made her teeth chatter.

When they arrived, Margot waited by the door."Thank God, you're here! "

"Where is the girl?" Eulalia asked.

"Come, she's in my bed," Margot said.

They left Pedro standing by the door.

The two women flew to the girl's bedside. Alana's eyes were closed. A soft groan escaped her light-coloured lips.

"It hurts, Mama" Her voice was barely audible. "What's happening to me? Maybe I'm dying, I don't want to die!"

"How long has she been bleeding?" Eulalia asked.

"A couple of hours. It's worse now, and doesn't stop."

The old woman rubbed her palms."And it won't until we do something."

"What do you mean?" Margot asked.

"No time to talk. Get me a basin and soap. I also need clean rags."

Margot hurried to do what she was asked. When she came back, Alana's legs were splayed as Eulalia rubbed the girl's lower stomach. "Stay by your daughter's side, hold her hand, and talk to her. This is going to hurt."

Eulalia put a few rags under the girl's bottom. She kept rubbing Alana's lower abdomen vigorously while muttering an incantation.

Alana screamed as Eulalia reached between the girl's legs

and took out a small red mass. The old woman wrapped her findings in a rag and put it on the floor.

Margot's hands shook uncontrollably. "And if the bleeding doesn't stop, what am I supposed to do?"

"You must take her to the town's clinic. They'll know how to help her."

"I'll make sure my girl is safe."

Before leaving the room Eulalia said, "Don't forget to bury the little thing. It should go back to the earth."

* * *

Alana's recovery took a few days. Too long for her liking. Her mother fussed over her, making soups, preparing her favourite dishes, and suspending her chores.

Margot entered the kitchen carrying a covered bowl. "Amor, you should eat this."

She placed the bowl in front of her daughter.

"What's it?" Alana asked, wrinkling her nose.

"Something to help you recover your strength. It's called *Nachi.*" Margot uncovered the bowl, and the red gelatinous contents shook in her hands. She thought of her own mother giving her Nachi "to help you to be strong and healthy,"she'd said. Margot disliked it, but with time, she learned to eat it because of its curative effects.

"I don't care what it's called. What's in it?" Alana asked.

"Goat's blood. Just have a little bit. Please, amor, try it."

Alana closed her eyes, opened her mouth, and swallowed a spoonful of congealed goat blood. She took a deep breath.

Through her red lips and teeth, she said, "I think I'm going to vomit."

She didn't.

* * *

A warm breeze played with Alana's hair as she strode to school. Her percale dress, a tad too small, outlined her changing figure. She stopped to pick wildflowers.

Unexpectedly, Alana's pulse quickened when she heard the water tumble over the pebbles in the nearby creek. *Why does this place scare me? Have I been here before? It feels familiar like I should remember but can't.*

Turning away from the creek, she stared at the forested path and ran the rest of the way to school.

"Good morning, children." Manuel stood in front of the class.

"Good morning, teacher," they answered in unison.

"Be seated," He gazed at the flowers on his desk.

"Those are beautiful. Who brought them?"

"My sister did," said little Marcia.

Manuel glanced at a blushing Alana. "Thank you."

When the class ended, Manuel approached her and crouched beside her desk. "I'm

glad you're back in school. You look well."

"I was sick, but I'm fine now," Alana said, looking down.

Manuel felt relieved."Ah, I see. Welcome back. If you need help with your work, let me know." He stood up. "You may go now."

Every time I'm close to Don Manuel, my heart beats faster and I feel flushed. Is that what people call love? I wouldn't know, but I like the feeling.

Alana left the classroom and went to meet her siblings playing nearby.

* * *

Margot sat on a kitchen bench, peeling potatoes for dinner. Pedro came back from the orchard with ripe tomatoes and lettuce. He sat by her side. She smiled and touched his hand, feeling content with having her husband home. It felt nice to hear his breathing beside her at night. It gave her a sense of comfort.

She stood to face him. "Alana's feeling much better. She went back to school today."

Pedro rubbed his chin. "She was with child. Wasn't she?"

Margot fixed her gaze on him. "We should be grateful she lost the pregnancy. Thanks to

Eulalia, Alana's alive." She kept going, "Everything that happened is in the past now. Life must go on."

"If you say so." Pedro shook his head.

Margot sensed her husband was agreeing to calm her down, but in his heart, the pain of her daughter's assault remained hidden.

She sat beside Pedro and looked into his blue eyes. "Alana is going to finish school this year. We have to talk about her future. But we need to know what she thinks first," Margot said.

"What?" He frowned and raised his voice. "She's a child. We know what's best for her. We don't need her opinion."

Alana skipped into the kitchen. "Is dinner ready, Mama?"

"Soon, amor, soon."

Pedro looked stern. "Sit down. We need to talk." His eyes focused on Alana.

Shit, Dad is pissed. "What did I do?"

Margot tried to hide a little smile. "Nothing, amor. We need to talk about what you want to do when school is done."

"I already know. I want to be a teacher, like Don Manuel."

"No. You need to stay at home to help your mother. Later, you are going to look for a job in town." Pedro said.

"But Papa, I want to go to the teacher's school!" she cried out.

"Alana, don't be disrespectful to your father," Margot said.

Pedro couldn't control his rage and pounded the table. "I'll decide what you do after school!"

"Listen to me both of you, please. Let's talk this over," Margot pleaded.

Alana left the kitchen crying. "I hate you both!"

* * *

The next day at school, Alana's withdrawn attitude concerned Manuel. Her pale face and puffy eyes gave it away.

"You seem distracted today. We could talk during recess if you want to."

"I'd like that."

A little later on the school patio, Alana sat on a bench under a tree. Manuel joined her.

"You want to tell me what's bothering you?"

"It's my parents. They don't get me. They want me to go to town and find a job when school is finished. But, I don't want to."

"What do you want to do?"

"I want to be a teacher, like you."

Manuel's eyes sparkled and gleamed."I'm glad to know you want to be a teacher. But, don't do it because of me. Do it because it's important to you."

Alana chewed on her bottom lip. "Well... Maybe it was just a dream."

"You should pursue your dreams. Always."

Alana glanced at Manuel. Her cheeks became rosy and her heart thumped in her chest.

He stood and cleared his throat. "It's time to go back to class."

* * *

At night, after dinner, Manuel cleared the table while Fernando wove a wicker basket to sell at the town's market.

"Finish your work later. We need to talk." Manuel's voice sounded rough.

"Am I in trouble? Did I do something wrong?"

"I'm not sure. I need to know the truth about your encounter with Alana."

Fernando left the basket and stood behind an empty seat. He placed his hands on the back of the chair, "I already told you what happened."

"Tell me again."

"What's the point? You'll think I'm lying, anyway." Fernando's knuckles turned white as he gripped the chair.

"You told me you tried to kiss her, she slapped you and you left. If that is the truth, I'll accept it" Manuel looked straight into the boy's eyes. He wanted to believe in his brother's innocence.

"It's true," Fernando said. "May I go back to my basket?"

"Do what you have to," he mumbled.

Manuel went outside, ran his fingers through his hair and sighed. Evenings were so pleasant in the country. The treetops swayed with the breeze carrying the countryside aromas. His small corn plantation and the orchard thrived. When winter arrived, the greenery would become dormant until next spring. He realized life is all about adjusting to change.

Manuel returned to the kitchen to talk to his brother. "I want to tell you something. I finished my teaching contract here and I've been offered a position in the city. What do you think?"

"Ah, I don't know what to say." Fernando bit his lower lip, then he shrugged.

"I'd like to teach in the city. You could get a good job there too," Manuel said.

"Maybe we should go, then."

The following day, after classes Manuel asked Alana to stay. "I won't keep you for long. But I need to share some news with you. I got a new job in the city."

She stared at him. "What? When are you going? What am I going to do without you? I mean... what's the school going to do without you?"

"You'll have a nice new teacher. Fernando and I are leaving in a couple of weeks."

She pushed back tears."I'm happy for you, Don Manuel," she said without conviction. "I wish you well. We'll miss you here at school."

"Thank you, Alana." He wanted to touch her hand, but he didn't dare.

* * *

Manuel and Fernando moved to the city, and into a good lodging arrangement within a family's home. The place had a guest house at the back of the property. It was small but comfortable.

Fernando got a job as an apprentice in a shoe shop, where the owner, an old man with a long white beard and inquisitive eyes, chose to give the boy a chance. Gratitude filled Manuel's heart toward the old man's generous approach to his brother.

Manuel started his new job. The boarding school was large compared with his two-room rural school. The building had a particular colonial aspect, with its white stucco walls, red-clay tiles and rustic appearance.

The first floor had a couple of rooms for teachers and several other classrooms. Its second floor held dormitories for students coming from the interior. It was obvious the place had seen better times and required some upkeep. Nevertheless, it served its purpose. The school staff consisted of three other teachers who greeted him in a friendly manner.

After a long while, Manuel had the impression things were falling into place. Except he couldn't shake his doubts about Fernando's involvement in Alana's attack, in spite of telling his brother he believed him.

* * *

Time passed and Alana graduated from her country school. She had always enjoyed going to classes and learning, as shown by her excellent academic performance. Her determination to become a teacher had been on her mind for a long time and her mother supported her idea. As always, she took her daughter's side.

They finished dinner and Margot put the dishes away. The sweet smell of ripe plums permeated the kitchen, as she had prepared jam that morning. Margot stood behind Pedro's chair, caressed his head, and sat beside him.

"Alana is getting her bags ready for tomorrow. She'll be taking the first bus to the city. You should talk to her."

Pedro's brow wrinkled. "Maybe she should come and talk to me."

"She is as stubborn as you are."

"She knows I don't like her leaving home. But I talked to my sister anyway, didn't I? Laura'll be waiting for her."

"Sure. Let's hope she is kind to Alana. We know your sister can be difficult at times."

"Yes. But, she had accepted to board her niece for a fee and that's good," he said.

Margot nodded. "Alana's going to be here any minute. Please, be patient with her."

Pedro set his jaw. "I'll try. But she better mind her words."

After arranging her hair in a ponytail, Alana entered the kitchen.

"Have a seat," said Pedro.

Alana wrung her fingers and she hid her hands under her thighs. "I want to thank you for talking to Aunt Laura. I'll do my best to get along."

"You better. You'll be a guest in her house."

"I don't want to leave like this." She stood and faced Pedro. "You know I love you, Papa, even if we don't always agree on everything."

"I know." His eyes brightened. "I wish you well. I hope you'll be a good teacher."

"I'll try my best, Papa."

"Alana is not going to the end of the world," Margot tried to smile." She'll come to visit often, right amor?

"Si, Mama."

Margot kissed her daughter's cheek. With her right hand, she made the sign of the cross on Alana's forehead, saying: "I'm giving you my benediction." The same ritual her mother, her grandmother, her great-grandmother and all the mothers of the village bestowed on their children, to protect them from evil and bring them good luck.

"Gracias, Mama," Alana said.

Margot smiled."You should go to bed. You have to get up early tomorrow."

As Alana left the kitchen, Margot turned to Pedro and touched his cheek. "Thanks, love,"

she said, and without waiting for his reaction, she left the room.

From her bedroom window, under the pale glow of a distant moon, Alana gazed at the stars. She crossed her arms over her chest and took a deep breath. Excitement about going away filled her heart, but at the same time, she felt concerned about the unknown, about leaving her family and all she knew and loved.

* * *

The following day, it was a cold Sunday morning. When Alana stepped off the bus, her inquiring eyes absorbed the newness of the place. A cacophony of a few cars, street vendors and horse-drawn carriages trotting on the cobbled street assaulted her ears. She had seen a car once before, but she couldn't take her eyes off that amazing machine. All that noise felt alien, as the peace and quiet of the countryside remained engraved in her brain.

A strong smell of manure, overripe fruits and debris by the side of the road made it hard to breathe. The chorus of vendors shouting their products added to the chaos of the place.

The city looks so big compared to my country village. There are many buildings, shops, strip malls, and townhouses. How will I survive in this 'jungle'?

Aunt Laura lived in an old colonial house. Its tall, white, peeling walls and dark metal-barred windows looked so different from the bright blue colours of Alana's country home. She knocked, and after a few minutes, an old lady wearing a black shawl opened the door.

"Hello, Aunt Laura. Do you remember me? I'm Alana."

Countless wrinkles covered the older woman's face. A few strands of white hair hung loosely from under her woolen hat. Her small cat-looking eyes scanned the newcomer.

"Hello, Alana. Don't you stand there, come in. It's getting cold." Alana followed her into the kitchen.

“I was going to have soup. Do you want some?”

“I’d love some. Thanks.” She opened her bag and took out a large piece of cheese, a dozen eggs, and some fruit and put them on the kitchen table. “Mama sent these for you.”

"Good," her aunt said, without looking at her or the bundle of foods.

They ate their soup in silence.

After they finished eating, Laura said, “I’ll show you the place I’ve prepared for you.”

Alana followed her aunt to the end of a large corridor."It’s not much but I think you’ll have what you need," Laura opened the door and left.

The room was large, crowded and filled with old furniture and things not being used anymore. In a corner, a small bed, a flimsy bedside table and an old desk made up her “bedroom.” A musty smell permeated the room. Alana opened the creaky window and exhaled.

Despite the clutter, Alana was happy the house had an indoor toilet and running water. No more trips to the well.

* * *

The following day Alana got up, had breakfast, and left the house. As she rode the bus,

she wondered about what the future may hold in this new place.

When she arrived at her college, dozens of young people filled the corridors of the large building , some looking for classrooms, some chatting and some holding hands like toddlers. Alana walked down a school corridor, her hands in her jacket's pockets. Coming from a small country town, large crowds made her uneasy.

The three-story building looked imposing with its ample corridors and large classrooms. The main floor had an amphitheater-like structure where students met. A buzzing noise filled the large space. Some students talked out loud or laughed while others greeted friends they hadn't seen since the last term.

On the second floor, the first-year teaching program occupied a few classrooms. The

third floor housed older students. Alana located the administration office, searched for her assigned place, and found her classroom. She went in and sat in a discreet corner.

Her first class was about to start. An older lady who wore her white hair in a bun at the base of her neck and a pair of glasses on the tip of her nose welcomed the students. The teacher explained what was expected of them, including their commitment to hard work. Alana listened attentively. An uncomfortable feeling of apprehension took hold of her.

Sitting beside her another student doodled on her notepad. The girl turned around, "Hi, I'm Carmen. A lot to take in on the first day, right?"

"Hi, I'm Alana. Yes, I'm nervous already."

"Don't be. My sister is in her second year. She said if you show up for classes and do your work, you'll be fine."

Alana and Carmen had similar courses, shared their lunch hours, and soon became good friends.

* * *

As weeks went by, Alana's aunt's behaviour changed. The girl wondered why her Aunt Laura acted that way. *She's so cranky and irritable. Maybe she prefers to live alone. Do I make her feel uncomfortable?*

Once, when Alana came back to the house in the evening after a full day of attending classes, Laura was waiting for her.

"You're late," her aunt said as Alana entered the kitchen.

"I'm so sorry. I had a very busy day."

"I don't want to hear your excuses. If you aren't home on time, there'll be no dinner."

"I don't want supper. Thanks. I already ate," she lied. Alana excused herself, went to her room, and cried.

The following evening she was writing a paper when Laura entered her room."It's late. You should turn your light off."

"Sorry, but I have to finish this paper for tomorrow."

"Too bad. Electricity isn't free, you know?"

She sighed. "That's fine, Aunt."

Sometimes college classes ended late in the evenings. On those days, Alana didn't get dinner and went to bed hungry. As time passed, her aunt's behaviour worsened.

One day, after classes, she talked about her situation with Carmen.

"I don't know what to do. She is a bitter old woman, and I'm not welcome at her place."

"My boarding house is going to have a room available at the end of the month. You should move out and leave that ogre alone," Carmen said.

Alana had to put up with her aunt's biting remarks for a couple of weeks. Finally, unwilling to take any further abuse, she wrote to her parents explaining her need to move out.

* * *

Back in the country, after dinner, Margot and Pedro sat outside their home, facing the old weeping willow. For a short while, Margot reminisced about the first time Pedro kissed her under a willow, a lifetime ago.

She shook her head. More important matters needed her attention. "I got a letter from Alana. You want to read it?" She withdrew the letter from her apron's pocket and handed it to Pedro. He didn't take it.

"Tell me what she says. You know I'm not too good at reading things."

"Alana's having problems at Laura's home," Margot said.

"How come?"

"Your sister has been unkind to her. She made her feel unwelcome in many ways. She denies Alana dinner when she has late classes."

Pedro cracked his knuckles. "I'm sending Laura money to have Alana at her place. This isn't charity."

"Alana is very unhappy. We need to help her."

Margot didn't have to convince Pedro to accept their daughter's decision to leave her aunt's place.

* * *

Alana dreaded going home to Laura's for what was coming. As usual, no dinner for her because of being late. It didn't matter anymore.

In the kitchen, Laura was rinsing her plate in the sink.

"Sorry, Aunt. Could we talk?"

"You're late again. Dinner was already served."

"I'm not hungry."

"What do you want then?"

"I have to tell you something. I've found a place closer to the college. I'm moving. It's better for me."

The old lady's eyes widened. "How're you going to pay your rent?"

"I'm going to work plus with the money Papa used to send you, I'll make do."

"I thought you liked my company. I didn't know you were unhappy in my house."

Alana kept silent.

Laura insisted, "I tried to make you feel comfortable, but you are too hard to please." She scowled at the girl. "You little ingrate. I'm glad you'll be out of my home."

"Sorry, you feel that way, Aunt." She turned around and left the kitchen.

* * *

Alana moved to her new boarding house. Her bedroom was cozy and bright, with a big window overlooking a veggie garden. A good-size bed occupied the centre of the room. An old fashion lamp sat atop the bedside table, a desk and a chair, completed the room's decor. She took a deep breath, swirled around with her arms stretched out and smiled.

After a couple of weeks, Carmen helped her to find a job at the bakery where she worked. Alana worked three evenings a week, making enough money to supplement what her father sent monthly.

One evening, as she was ready to close the shop, a customer came in.

"Hello, may I have some bread, please?" he asked.

Alana thought she had heard that voice before. She turned around and froze. Her heart raced and her throat tightened.

"Don Manuel, I can't believe it's you!"

"Hello, Alana. What a nice surprise!" His voice shook when he spoke. "What are you doing here?"

"I work here."

"I wasn't expecting to see you. How are you?"

"Fine. I'm attending a teacher's school. I finished my first semester."

"That's very good. I'm so glad you're pursuing your dream." He paused to control his emotion. "I'd love to talk to you a bit more. When you're not working, would you like to go for a walk?"

Her eyes became brighter. "I'd love to."

Back at his place, Manuel couldn't figure out how to ask Alana the question that has been burning in his mind for so long. But he had to. The matter had to be discussed.

The rest of the week dragged on for Alana, waiting for Manuel to come by the bakery. She was wiping the counter when he came in.

"Hello, Alana."

"Hi, Don Manuel. I'm happy to see you."

"Please, don't call me Don anymore. I'm not your teacher. You're a grown-up now."

"I couldn't call you any other way. You've been my teacher for as long as I can remember."

"That's fine. Call me whatever you want. I don't mind. Are you working tomorrow?"

"No. The shop doesn't open on Saturdays."

"I see. If you are not busy, would you like to go out? We could go to the movies if you want."

Her heart fluttered." Yes. I love going to the movies."

* * *

The next day, they went to the movies and watched an old black-and-white film featuring Charlie Chaplin. The actor's funny faces and happy ending to the story made Alana laugh and lifted her spirit.

Manuel looked serious. Alana gave him a side glance and her smile transformed his stern face for a moment. "You didn't like the movie, Don Manuel?"

"Oh, no. I liked it."

After the movie, they went for ice cream and a stroll in the park. Manuel took a deep breath. "I need to ask you something. May I?"

"Sure." She licked her ice cream.

"Do you remember when you finished grade school?"

"Yes. It's been over a year."

"You recalled when you were sick and missed school for a few days?"

"Yes. I think so. Why?"

He dried his sweaty palms on the side of his pants. "Because something terrible happened to you."

"What are you saying?" Alana wrinkled her forehead.

"Someone attacked you on your way to school. Don't you remember?"

"I don't know what you are talking about."

"After the attack, you got sick, and your mother looked after you. Don't you recall that either?"

"I think I had some problems. My mind was fussy. I don't recall much."

"I need you to remember. Please, Alana." With his

fingers, he dried the drops of perspiration running down his temples.

"Why? I don't understand."

"Please, make an effort. Close your eyes and try to remember the attack."

"What? I don't remember any attack. Why are you doing this?"

Manuel didn't answer. Squeezing his eyes, he shook his head.

"Calm down, Don Manuel. What's wrong with you?" Alana touched his arm.

"I think I better go," he said and left her sitting on the bench.

She stayed thinking about what Manuel had said. *An attack? On my way to school? I should remember. Shouldn't I?*

* * *

The sweet smell of wildflowers greeted Alana when she descended from the bus. Springtime carried its colours and aromas, bringing with it warm feelings of her childhood. It had been a year since she left home and excitement about seeing her family filled her heart. Even though she enjoyed the city, the country was her home. Its dusty road brought to her mind memories of her younger years. Nostalgia invaded her soul.

In the distance, she saw her house, with its terracotta-coloured tiles, blue-rimmed windows, the orchard, and the old willow. The familiarity of the scene overwhelmed her with joy.

She got off the bus and ran to her mother, melting in her arms.

"Oh, my sweet girl," Margot said, "I'm so happy you are home." She kissed Alana's cheeks.

"Me too, Mama, I've missed you so much."

"I've missed you more." Drying her tears with her old shawl, Margot said, "Your father and the children are waiting for you at home. Let's go."

"Si, Mama." She grabbed her worn wicker bag, and held hands with her mother as they walked home.

Pedro stood at the house entrance, while the children made a fuss shouting, "Alana is home. She's home!"

"Welcome, Alana." Pedro said and hugged her tightly. "It's good you're here."

"I'm happy to be home, Papa."

Pedro glanced at his daughter's teary eyes. He came closer and kissed her forehead.

After a special dinner, Margot had prepared for the occasion, the family stayed in the kitchen talking to Alana, asking about life in the city, her friends, and her school.

The next day, she woke up late. Margot was already working in the orchard.

"Good morning, Mama."She kissed her mother on both cheeks.

Sweat ran down Margot's face, and she dried it with her forearm. "Good morning, amor. You slept well?"

"Yes, I did. I need to talk to you about something important."

"What is it, darling?"

"Could we talk when you are done working?"

"I'm done for now. Let's go."

They left the orchard and sat under the shade of the old willow.

"I saw Don Manuel a couple of weeks ago," Alana said.

"Oh, that's nice. How is he doing?"

"He is fine." The girl twisted her thumbs nervously.

"Tell me, what's troubling you," Margot asked.

Alana told her about the conversation with Manuel; Margot's face dropped in shock. Struggling for control, she felt dizzy. Her pallid face scared Alana.

"Mama, are you well? You look so pale."

"Don't worry, love. I'm just tired. Please, go on."

"He told me something had happened to me when I was on my way to school, last year. He said somebody attacked me. I don't remember any of that. What's he talking about, Mama?"

Fear settled in Margot's heart. Her voice quavered when she spoke. "I have no idea. I don't know why he's making up those stories. If something had happened to you, I should have known, right? I'm your mother, so believe me. Nothing happened to you."

"Si, Mama. I trust you. I'm happy we talked." She kissed her and went back to the house.

While in her room, Alana thought about the conversation with Margot. *Mom looked*

nervous. Was she lying? No, not my mother. Was Don Manuel making up stories? But why?

Margot stayed behind under the willow. She covered her face with both hands and tried to make sense of what was happening. She couldn't comprehend why Don Manuel talked to Alana about the attack after such a long time. What purpose did it serve?

* * *

Back in the city, night arrived carrying its darkness and silence. The same blackness reigned in Manuel's heart since his conversation with Alana. He felt their talk was useless. She didn't remember the incident, even when he tried to push her to do so.

What was he supposed to do? Keep living with the uncertainty of Fernando's culpability? The boy denied the attack. But, did he know his brother at all?

Manuel went to bed, trying to hide his doubts, but his mind wouldn't be still. *To get any peace, I have to know the truth about Alana's attack. I want to believe my brother is innocent but, is he?*

. . .

The next morning, a faint ray of sunshine peeked through the bedroom window illuminating Manuel's face.

The new day found him brooding over the whole situation. He lay in bed, eyes opened, fingers laced behind his head as he thought.

After breakfast, Manuel said to his brother, "I need to talk to you."

"Sure. What about?" The boy sat in a relaxed posture, leaning back, an arm hooked over the back of the chair.

"We have to talk about what happened to Alana. Last year, in the country."

The boy looked his brother straight in the eyes. "I didn't attack her, I just tried to kiss her, nothing else. I wish she was here to answer your questions." He stared at his feet. "What can I do to make you believe me?"

Manuel clenched his jaw and shook his head.

Fernando stood still. He opened up his shirt to take out a plain silver crucifix hanging from his neck and showed it to Manuel. His voice wavered when he spoke, "Mama gave me this when she got sick. She said if I wore it, she'd always be with me. I swear on Mama's memory, I didn't attack Alana." His eyes welled as he kissed the crucifix.

Manuel stared at his brother in amazement. He was astonished and confused as he tried to take in what had just happened.

All this time, Manuel had doubted Fernando. All the pain he'd endured had been for nothing. His brother wasn't guilty of Alana's assault! When Fernando kissed the crucifix Manuel understood he wasn't lying.

The two brothers locked in a strong embrace. Words were not needed, they stayed holding each other, their hearts beating in unison.

* * *

The small church stood on the outskirts of the city. The chapel was empty, except for a man kneeling in a pew. Deep wrinkles covered his face. His shrunken eyes showed sorrow and discontent. His mouth was a tight line. Head bowed, he prayed; the beads of his green and pale blue rosary moved slowly through his withered fingers.

In the center of the altar, a large crucifix depicted the image of Christ. Silence reigned. The aroma of incense spread through the place. An old priest came out from the back of the church, walked toward the altar, bowed, and entered the confessional.

The man on the pew stood and followed the priest. He knelt by the enclosed stall.

"Bless me, Father, for I have sinned," the man said.

"Tell me, son."

"I committed a crime, and I don't want to carry this burden any longer. I need God to forgive me." The man blinked back tears.

"What have you done, son?"

His voice broke, "I assaulted a girl last year."

"That's a terrible sin. Was the girl someone you knew?"

"No, Father. In the country, I went from place to place working in the fields. I've never returned to that village. I don't even remember the girl's face." He dropped his chin to his chest.

"Why did you do it, son?"

"I don't know why," he paused for a minute, then he said, "Yes, I know. Because I was a drunk lustful animal." He covered his face with both hands and cried.

"Have you done it again?"

Between sobs, he answered, "No, Father, I swear to God."

"You can't lie in God's church," the priest said.

"I'm telling the truth. I've mended my ways. I'm married and we were expecting a child, but God punished me for my sin, and we lost our baby. But, I can't forgive myself for what I did to that poor girl. Do you think God could forgive me?"

"God is merciful. If your repentance is sincere, He'll listen to your plea."

"What should I do, Father?"

"Be a good Christian, follow the Commandments, pray for forgiveness, be a compassionate human being, and look after your family. With time, you may find peace in your heart."

The priest gave the man his penance, placed his palms together, closed his eyes, and prayed. When he opened the confessionary's door, the man was gone.

* * *

Margot wrapped her poncho around her shoulders and knocked at Eulalia's hut. Despite her cover, she shivered. She hadn't seen the medicine woman in about a year.

"Hello, Margot. This is a surprise. Come in."

"Hello, Eulalia. I brought you eggs, fresh fruit, and corn."

The old woman displayed her toothless smile. "Thank you. Sit by my side. Do you want some tea?

"No, thanks."

"What do you need from me?"

"I'm here because I need your help," Margot pleaded. She told Eulalia that Manuel talked to her daughter about the attack and his intent to make Alana remember the incident.

"It won't happen. The potion I gave her erased from Alana's mind any memories of the incident. Forever."

Pacing the earthen floor, Margot wrapped her shawl over her shoulders. Nervously, she asked, "What should I do, Eulalia?"

The witch smiled gently. "I don't have all the answers, you know. But someone does."

Margot looked puzzled. "Who?"

"The Pachamama, Mother Earth. She's all-knowing. She told me what potion to give to your daughter and what root to offer her to lose her pregnancy. Now, she'll tell me what to do about you."

When she was a little girl, Margot's mother and grandmother had spoken to her about the Pachamama, a goddess revered by the indigenous people of the Andes who presides over planting, harvesting and embodies the mountains. The Pachamama allowed miracles to occur, but only some chosen beings were able to conjure her spirit. Eulalia was born with those powers.

"I thought The Pachamama was a folktale," Margot said. "Maybe a superstition or something people had made up or heard of."

"No. The Pachamama is as real as you and me. Who do you think gives us sunny days to lift our spirits, rain to feed our crops, or beautiful moon nights to encourage men and women to multiply? She does."

Margot said nothing.

The old woman brought a wooden box to the table and placed it in front of her visitor.

"What's in there?" Margot asked.

"Here is the answer to your question. Pebbles from the creek, the one that runs by the old weeping willow."

"I don't understand."

Eulalia emptied the box and stroked the pebbles. "They are so soft, the caress of the water through the times made them like that."

"What happens now?"

"Be quiet, woman." The witch closed her eyes and stood still relaxing her body. Her breathing became almost imperceptible while waiting for the spirit to come to her. After a few minutes, Eulalia, as if in a trance hummed a soft melody, moving her hands back and forth over the pebbles. A luminous halo surrounded Eulalia's whole body.

Margot witnessed the scene in awe.

When the witch opened her eyes, her pupils were dilated and a strange brightness radiated from them. "I have your answer," she said.

The old woman put the pebbles back in the box. She sat on her straw-bottom chair and rested her hands over her lap.

Margot waited expectantly.

"The pebbles have seen it all. They see and let the water follow its course, for you can't stay in the past. You have to let go of what you can't change."

The medicine woman stood and cupped Margot's face in her hands. "Your daughter

is fine. She won't remember a thing. She is ready to be a happy woman and you should too."

Margot dabbed her tears with the back of her hand.

"Allow yourself to let go. Like the pebbles under the old willow."

It was night when Margot left Eulalia's hut, her mind was still taking in what just had happened. A feeling of calmness and solace started to flourish in her heart.

The Pachamama was right, Eulalia said the goddess always is.

A full moon shone in the sky. It would be easy to find her way home to her family.

THE END

ACKNOWLEDGEMENTS

I have to express my gratitude to so many people that helped me in the long process to make my first short story collection a reality.

Thank you, Leslie Wibberly, my first reader from whom I've learned so much, thanks for your patience and guidance.

I'm grateful to my editors and friends, Jennifer Summersby and Margie Taylor, for their invaluable work.

To my Beta readers Annette Le Box, Nancy McNeil and Leslie Webberly; your help was greatly appreciated.

Special thanks to the talented Marie Mackay for the beautiful book cover.

My recognition to many writer's friends, Melanie Cossey, Lisa Hislop, Katherine Wagner and so many others for their input in some of my stories.

A big thank you to Ted Yabut Jr. and the Coquitlam

Writers Group, for their friendship, feedback and encouragement over the years.

And best for last: to my awesome family, Ramon, Alfonsina and Amanda; thank you for your guidance, support, and never-ending love.

ABOUT THE AUTHOR

Growing up in Chile, Margarita found inspiration in her family of writers and poets. Later on, she moved to Canada and after retiring from a long career as a nurse/ midwife, she decided to take on a new challenge; learning to write narrative and fiction in English.

In 2016 she started to write in her adopted tongue. This debut short story collection represents the work of six years. Several of her stories and articles have been published on Reedsy, a literary site and on Tint, an online literary journal dedicated to ESL creative writing.

Margarita lives in Vancouver with her husband. She enjoys spending time with her two adult daughters who live nearby.

Manufactured by Amazon.ca
Bolton, ON

34316151R00164